Nightwatching

Méira Cook

Nightwatching

HarperCollins*PublishersLtd*

Nightwatching
Copyright © 2015 by Méira Cook.
All rights reserved.

Published by HarperCollins Publishers Ltd

First Canadian edition

No part of this book may be used or reproduced in any manner whatsoever without the prior written permission of the publisher, except in the case of brief quotations embodied in reviews.

HarperCollins books may be purchased for educational, business, or sales promotional use through our Special Markets Department.

HarperCollins Publishers Ltd
2 Bloor Street East, 20th Floor
Toronto, Ontario, Canada
M4W 1A8

www.harpercollins.ca

Library and Archives Canada Cataloguing in Publication information is available upon request.

ISBN 978-1-44343-386-0

Printed and bound in the United States of America
RRD 9 8 7 6 5 4 3 2 1

For Mark

The summer Ruthie turned eleven was a strange one, a hot cracked thing one couldn't stare at full-on or walk down barefoot. The streets shimmered like water in the heat but it never rained or hardly ever, only quick swampy afternoon showers like darting presses of a steam iron that left the town strangely rumpled and gasping for air. And it was the summer, too, that Ruthie shot up, her bones all gangly from the shock and her skin jumpy also and nothing seemed to fit any more, not least of all her own body. Nights she couldn't sleep for the growing pains in her legs.

"Like a beanstalk," said Bettina Foley, the next door music teacher, who had been trying all spring to teach her "*Au clair de la lune*" and whose failure to coax attention from the fidgeting girl had made her grim and vicious.

"Sit *still*, child," she commanded huffily, "or do you have ants in your pants? Yes? No? Why, Ruthven, haven't I always told you that music cannot proceed from chaos? Harmony is, is . . ."

But harmony eluded Bettina Foley in the heat of the airless music room where the mantel clock ticked the afternoon off into equal intervals of sixty minutes each. Outside the veld rose and fell with the hum of the cicadas and the glare emptied the mind of all thoughts but the dash for shade and the longing for—oh Lord—a glass of something cold to wash away despondency.

The trouble with the Blackburn girl, as Bettina Foley confided to her good friend Annemarie Willems, was more than just growing pains. "Poor child," agreed Annemarie, helping herself to a soft centre from the box of Black Magic chocolates that they had purchased on entering the little cinema. The two women were attending a Saturday matinee; they were devoted fans of the bioscope and agreed that they were lucky indeed that first-run films arrived in the Free State town only a month or two after they came out in Johannesburg. Today was *The Towering Inferno*. Even with the anticipation of their all-time favourite movie actor, Mr. Paul Newman, in all his lazy, blue-eyed good humour, the music teacher couldn't help feeling that her friend had too swiftly dismissed the cause of her errant pupil's anomie.

"Well, but you see, my dear, one can't discount the psychology of the situation. Now the late Mr. Foley always used to say I had a way with psychology and in this case—why it's a textbook! First you have the dead mother and

Nightwatching

then you have the hard-working, handsome father who's at that Oedipal stage of life. Naturally the child is forlorn and betwixt and can't learn her piano, *try though I might*."

"Mmm." Her mouth softly plugged with melting chocolate, Annemarie had to content herself with nodding sagely and casting admiring looks upon her friend, though at length she was able to admit that it was a damn shame and that something should be done, natuurlik, and so on, and, and . . .

But the interval was over, the house lights dimmed and the opening credits began to roll. Eagerly the two women settled back to await the movie, the vast, nuzzling close-up of their inner lives projected on the slightly wavering screen of the downtown Palace Movie Theatre.

When Miriam wanted to punish Ruthie she just plain ignored her. Ruthie could take any amount of yelling from her teacher, Mrs. Bakkes, and the kids at school couldn't make her cry though they'd not yet given up trying. And on the three—was it?—occasions when her remote yet kindly father had had to do his stern duty by her and solemnly bend her over his knee, she had not cried though her heart had broken. But to Miriam, the Blackburn family maid of almost twelve years, the child was an open book.

Ruthie had once been a sturdy child but lately she had shot up in what seemed to be contrary directions, so that she was always moving, tapping a foot or rubbing at her high forehead, just to get comfortable. Now she seemed all edges, elbows and knees and the sharp bone of her ankles and wrists poking through. She had dirty-blond hair, and even though it was often clean and although she brushed it every night, this way and that, giving it the lashings it so dearly deserved, every morning it was back to being the limp, fly-away thing she despised. Her eyes were blue: "like your Mama's," Miriam had once told her, and that was all there was to it. Her father had grey eyes which were the colour of the highway travelling off into the distance, and Miriam's own eyes were dark brown. She was a plump, firm-fleshed woman with beautiful white teeth and high cheekbones and she had the graceful carriage of one who had spent her youth walking with a bundle of washing on her head and a child on her back. She was often gentle but she could be stubborn too, and the habit of keeping her own counsel was second nature to her.

"Miri," Ruthie wheedled now, using the old childhood name, "oh, Mims, won't you please please please?"

No answer.

"Dearest sweetest nicest Mims. Mims of my heart, Mims of all the world's goodness . . ."

Miriam, who had been sitting at the kitchen table reading her newspaper, made a great to-do of shuffling to her feet and clattering about with pots and pans—*boom, bang, swipe*, and be quiet *you!*

"But why won't you ask him, why?"

There were eggs in the pan now and oil, too much it looked like, and Miriam, who was an expert on how Ruthie liked her eggs scrambled, set about breaking all her own rules so that soon the yolks were oozy with grease and the whites were limp with indifference. To stop herself from weeping, for she would not, she would *not*, it was too soon in the battle for one thing and too late in the day for another, Ruthie blinked hard, harder, gulped at her glass of water till the lump in her throat had subsided some and scratched at the inside of her arm until she had drawn the wet ease of blood that always calmed as nothing else did.

"Well, I'm not going to eat this, Miriam, of that you can be certain," yelled Ruthie, growing meaner with every word but she couldn't stop herself, the words had soured like milk in her stomach; they had to come up. "And I'm not sorry for what I called you, I'm not because you *are* a Bantu. That's what your indigenous population group is. We learned it at school. I'm a European and you're a Bantu. It's as simple as that, no need to be cross. No need"—she drew herself up as she'd seen her father do—"no need to take umbrage, my girl."

"Ho, is that so, meisie, is that right?"

Ruthie was so relieved that Miriam had decided to talk to her again that she felt dizzy with gratitude and pierced through with hunger. She grabbed up a fork and began to shovel the stiffening eggs into her mouth.

But Miriam hadn't finished yet, far from it. She lowered herself by degrees of rustling fury into the creaking kitchen chair. With one tug she straightened her apron, with another she settled the knot at the back of her doek. She placed one palm upon the other and her eyes she used to look deep into the eyes of this ungrateful so-and-so, this child she had known for all of her life until this moment of wrongful name-calling.

"Well, my girl, tell me then, were you born in Europe?"

Ruthie remained stubbornly silent. Miriam knew she'd been born right here in Welkom. She had been in the family for as long as Ruthie could remember, possibly forever.

"Okay, not born in Europe then."

Miriam pretended to ponder the matter, which she did—Ruthie was used to the spectacle—with a great stroking of the chin and a series of deepening *hmm*'s which seemed to proceed from the back of the throat. When Miriam got like this there was no stopping her; she was a locomotive with a locomotive's casual pluck and at these times she must run down the steep incline of her own outrage.

"Not born but perhaps a visitor? Tell me, my girl, when was this last visit of yours? It must have been a quick one because the good Miriam who looks after young Ruthie over here barely missed her. Well, she's getting on all right, old Miriam, now her memory's gone, and soon she'll be no use to anyone. Set her out with the garbage for the dustbin boys to take away in the morning!"

Through the open kitchen window a musical scale climbed uneasily, then stalled on a wrong note. The two sat like this at the kitchen table for a spell—Miriam expectant and Ruthie repentant—but Ruthie did not know how to apologize, never had. Apology was the empty bucket within her and it drained every good feeling she had ever had and then some.

"Eat your scrambles," said Miriam, who knew what was what, almost everything about Ruthie anyway, for hadn't she been there since forever. But wouldn't you know it the way the child commenced to quibble—the eggs were cold and anyway too runny, the day was too hot for eating just yet, and besides she didn't find herself quite hungry, thank you—by which Miriam was given to understand that to the contrary, something was still gnawing at her. A problem had her between its jaws.

"Tcha, meisie, why don't you ask him yourself?"

"But you know, you *know* he doesn't listen to me!"

Miriam sighed. Always, but always, she must walk the daughter through the father's taciturn elsewhereness. He was not an unloving man, but he was laconic, curt even, and with an understanding that reached backwards and forwards in a small tight circumference like a man's shadow at noon. Remote some might call him, busybodies that they were, but he was a man of clean habits, and he loved his daughter. He loved her but he did not appear to want her to accompany him to the capital city of Bloemfontein some two hours away, where it was his habit to visit every month for a weekend, although more now that he had become a Rotarian.

Outside, the noise of the crickets in the veld was like the voice of the heat itself, a ragged saw to cut the afternoon in half. "E*x*cellent work, Dion," called the next-door music teacher, "you have ex*cee*ded yourself." Ruthie tossed her head in imitation, catching Bettina Foley's stiff little chin jab into the air and the flirtatious sideways glance she always aimed when bestowing some particular musical compliment. In Ruthie's case these were seldom deserved or distributed.

"Oh, Dion, you have ex*cee*ded yourself," she mimicked, "your music falls upon the ear like rain falling in a desert and making unto the flowers bloom. You have magical fingers, oh, Dion! Dion, tickle me with your magical fingers, hee hee hee."

"Suka wena, child!" Miriam tried not to laugh, failed, then sought to mask hilarity with false indignation. "Why you want to make fun of that boy, hmm? I tell you what, you practise a little instead of laughing, then maybe I don't have to hear such a racket during your lesson. Yes, go practise now, Miss Money-to-Burn, or I'll tell your father on you!"

With one coolly assessing glance Ruthie measured the distance between the dark and gloomy parlour with its upstanding piano and her Miriam, who, riled up though she was, would not tell her father on her—never had and never would—and she flung herself out of the kitchen and into the yard and down the driveway, where she paused only to yank her bike upright and then she was off and pedalling furiously down the service road. She was hoping to catch up to Dion, who was only a lousy kid of eight or so but better than no one on this endless afternoon during the worst summer of her life, probably the worst summer ever.

Soon enough she caught sight of him on the path in front of her, his slumped back and skinny legs. "Oh, Dion," she fluted, batting her lashes at him so strenuously that she wobbled dangerously and almost toppled. "Dion, Dion, Dion, you have exceeded all expectations, you are a Paganini of the keyboards, my little man, you have first-rate magic fingers."

Dion bent to pick up a stone but looked suddenly uncertain whether or not to fling it. A look of terrible misery occluded his features because he was too young—three years younger than Ruthie—to dissemble and because the world, it seemed to him then, had shrunk to the distance between his red sticking-out ears and the *knock knock knock* of his rib cage against that bird, his heart.

Well, he was not such a bad fellow, thought Ruthie, old Dion. Just hangdog and small for his age, somewhat, with a tendency to moon about the edges of the playground and a mama whose anxiety, when she was not suffering one of her spells, trimmed him down to her hard bright need. Suddenly Ruthie decided, in one of those generous impulses so characteristic of her, to forgive him for his prowess at the piano. It was well known that he was Mrs. Foley's star pupil; he had long ago mastered "*Au clair de la lune*" and was well into preparations for his Grade One examination.

"Well, my boy," she began in an avuncular tone, "and where are you off to on this fine afternoon? Salubrious," she clarified, having always liked the euphony of this particular word.

No answer.

"The Caffy?" she hazarded. "Because I've got ten cents and if you've got, say, fifteen we can split a cream soda. Two straws. Separate turns but me first." Ruthie was by this time pedalling after Dion, who had turned and, his little music satchel dragging at his shoulders, was lurching along the service road, his head down.

"I called first and anyway I'm older."

No answer. Dion shuffled along digging his hands deeper in his pockets and the silence threatened to overbalance her, threatened to tip her off her bike and onto the road, when Dion said, "If I've got fifteen cents and you've got ten cents, why are you first?"

The two trudged along—Ruthie had to hop off her bike and dawdle beside him since he'd slowed now to the pace of his thoughts—while the boy examined the proposed transaction once again from every angle. "But you were first last time," he whined, "and the time before."

Ruthie sighed. "I'm just older than you," she told him wearily. "I'm older than you."

Ruthie had turned eleven at the beginning of that summer and was given a party dress by her father, who bought it from Mr. Kurtz, Kurtz Fashions, and by the last month of the summer the armholes were too tight and the hem had crept up the length of her legs and it was an embarrassment to be seen in. That's the kind of summer it was. Bright pink too, that dress, colour of sucked Valentine's hearts.

"Well," she sighed, blowing her damp fringe out of her eyes, "well, I am *fit* to be tied."

It was the habit of Ruthie and Miriam to listen to the radio in the afternoon and in particular a serial named *For Infamy and Bliss*, a soap whose black-hearted heroine was so far beyond the compass of decent moral conduct that Ruthie and Miriam never ceased to marvel at the myriad men who seemed unable to resist her. Now Ruthie gazed into the middle distance and tapped her foot. She looked over at Miriam hopefully but Miriam was busy at a much despised task, that of emptying the fly saucers on the windowsills. With fastidious fingers she tipped each saucer of syrupy fly slush down the outside drain, then rinsed the saucers. Soon she must mix up a new batch of sugar water in which she would float chunks of ripe watermelon to attract the flies, but, ah, not yet. Sighing, huffy with the heat, Miriam decided to boil up the kettle for a pot of hot tea to cool herself down.

"Miriam?"

"Mmm?"

"Miriam, which would you rather have—thousands of false lovers or just one true lover? Because I'd rather have thousands of false lovers, for sure. For *sure*. What we're talking about here is a hundred times a hundred and—no, but remember, *thousands* plural. I think it's a mistake to be distracted by so-called quality when we're dealing with volume of this magnitude."

"Tcha, what do you know about love, you mad child?"

"Volume of this magnitude," repeated Ruthie dreamily, for this was the summer that she fell in love with words, all kinds, plucking them out of the air and off the radio and cutting them whole cloth from the conversations she heard around her with little regard for meaning or nuance but loving the heat of them as they formed in her mouth and the surprise they caused on the faces of the adults around her, who might smile or nod or shake their heads at her precocity but who invariably noted their passing to her father.

"Ho, Lionel," her dad's partner, Mr. Feinstein, was always saying, "that's a fine gel you have there. A real firecracker!"

"Tune in to our serial this time again Monday afternoon," the radio announcer was advising, and Ruthie reached to snap him off mid-voice before he could try to play Pat Boone or Johnny Mathis or Gé Korsten at them, all of whom would put Miriam in a funk until doomsday. Sometimes Miriam would fiddle about until she got an African radio station playing jazz, but it was too hot that summer and they seldom listened to music anymore. But today, especially, some palliative was needed to while away the heavy afternoon, for her father had left early for Bloemfontein. They'd never doubted he would, but his refusal to just this very once allow his daughter to accompany him still rankled.

"Don't sulk now, Ruthie, there's a girl. I'll bring back something nice. Do the kids still collect comic books?" Then he'd reversed down the gravel drive without even a brief wave in the direction of his rear-view mirror, and Ruthie, standing by the service road, had only been able to count to *fifteen Mississippi* before the tail lights of his bottle-green Valiant disappeared entirely.

"Bloody," she remarked now in the suddenly still kitchen and Miriam merely nodded, *uh*-huh, unroused, as Ruthie had known she would be for Miriam never minded plain talk, though about blasphemy she was unbending. Ruthie took down the cards and began to shuffle. She was teaching Miriam to play Spite and Malice. Ruthie's best friend, Trudy Mason, had taught her this game at school last term and then she and Trudy had had a falling-out, she hardly knew why but the incident had left such a sore place in her soul that she had resolutely turned her thoughts from it and it was only now, at the tail end of the summer holidays, that she could bear to play the game that had once given her such pleasure. She would never have another friend.

Miriam cut and Ruthie dealt and they began to lay the cards out in the prescribed manner, Ruthie keeping a careful eye on her opponent's game for she was a scrupulous teacher and an honest broker. The kitchen door was propped open to let in whatever errant breeze might pass by, and every now and then Miriam would take up a palm fan and wave it about to redistribute the flies that rose, hovered for a moment buzzing, then dropped onto the sticky oilcloth of the kitchen table or the puddled tea leaves in the sink or the crumbs by the bread bin. And it seemed to Ruthie that each time, this happened more slowly: Miriam's fattish arms jiggling loosely in their short sleeves, the woven fan, the flies rising in a cloud, then settling one by one on this surface or that, until it seemed that the next time this occurred or the time after that, everything would stop altogether, everything would just stop.

"Three, two, one, spite," said Ruthie, rousing herself.

"*Uh*-huh," said Miriam, looking around for an opening but not briskly, and flapping at the front of her overalls to cool herself down. "Ho, girl, help me find a place for this jack, okay."

Miriam never could get it into her head that the game was not a team effort and Ruthie had almost given up trying to goad the competitive spirit in her. Now the two bent over the table with its bright playing cards in their wavy rows and the flies that had begun to settle once more, but before a place could be found for the jack they heard a slur of footsteps in the concrete yard and there was Sip. He'd been making a nuisance of himself that summer, sneaking away every chance he got and hot-footing it to the Blackburns' kitchen where he hung about, first in corners, then underfoot and finally pulling up a seat, bold as brass, to the kitchen table, where he sat now staring at Ruthie with his round, long-lashed child's eyes, tender with approbation. He was dark enough to disappear into the kitchen shadows and he could hold himself still and small yet alert.

"Goodness, Sipho, is that you?" Miriam would say, pretending surprise. Or perhaps there was no pretence involved, perhaps she *was* surprised, and every time. But Ruthie never was.

Sip belonged to the next-door's live-in gardener. He was much too old to be living with his father, but there was no relative to whom the child could be sent. Yet he was such a wee chap that it was hoped his presence might pass unnoticed or at least unremarked, and so far it had. As for Sip's father, he was a fine enough fellow but not a chatterer, which might have been the reason Sip found himself drawn to the kitchen with its radio crackle and feminine bustle of this and that. But he was ingratiating, poor Sip, and Ruthie judged him sorely for it, hating his small-boy's need, his crush on her, the place he'd wheedled into Miriam's hers-alone heart.

Now she jumped up and purposefully joggled his chair on the way to the sink for a glass of water that she'd only just that moment felt the need of, thirst and spitefulness combining to tighten a hot, red slipknot about her throat. "Whew! Hot, hot, hot," she felt obliged to exclaim, for Miriam was cutting her an evil glance, and Ruthie even put one hand up to her brow and fumbled for a moment with her wrist against the damp skin of her high white forehead. She made sure she aimed a surreptitious kick at Sip on her way back, *Hah, you!*

Sip swallowed hard. He was small for his age but plucky. In fact no one knew exactly how old Sip was, not even his father, but the consensus was that he was about eight or nine and small for it. "Tcha, look at you, all bone and gristle," Miriam would say, ringing his scrawny wrist with her thumb and index finger and thumping another plate of pap and meat stew onto the table beside him. But eat as he might, shovelling the heaped plates of stew and pap, boiled mielies and pumpkin and wild spinach into his humming little body, Sip hadn't grown even an inch over the summer. Not as far as Ruthie could tell. And this not-growing habit of his was yet another grudge she held against him, as if his failure to thrive on the good food her father provided and that Miriam cooked were merely a whim, a peevish and ungrateful reply to the courtesy of their hospitality.

Now the boy slipped into Miriam's still-warm chair and studied the pattern of her playing cards. He ignored the false problem of her impossible jack and began a swift and skilful hand that captured Ruthie's attention in spite of herself. He was a quick study and naturally lucky, and he had turned himself into a pair of eyes all that week in an effort to learn the rudiments of the game that Ruthie set such store by. The little red kitchen clock with its peculiarly emphatic minute hand plucked twenty identical rounds off above their heads while Miriam huffed and fanned herself at the stove. She was cutting up chicken thighs and giblets for a stew, disjointing bones and tearing up pieces of pimply skin. Carrots and onions, some potatoes. Even in this heat they had to eat.

Outside the heat gathered to a head, then broke in a short, violent thunderstorm, convulsive as a sneeze, as soon over as it began. Afterwards it was no cooler than it had been—warmer if anything. That was the way things were that summer, maybe every summer; Miriam always forgot what it was like from one year to the next. It was the only way, she suspected, a person might be persuaded to sigh and shake her head, shrug, *uh*-huh, make her peace with the body's weariness, the spirit's even greater. From the corner of her eye she noticed Ruthie's surreptitious pat at her chest. That girl had been feeling for breasts since the start of the summer. Now either the child was pawing away at the idea of something so far from apparent that it was kinder to ignore her or she was feeling the poke and itch of the breast buds as they swelled. Hard to tell.

Ruthie patted herself down again, pat pat, like a man who has misplaced his wallet, and Sip left off his cards and forgot himself so far as to stare. *Stop fidgeting, meisie,* Miriam wanted to tell her, *you'll only make it worse.* But what this worse was she hardly liked to say; worse for the child Ruthie was trying to leave behind, perhaps, worse for the not-child she was trying to become. And Miriam had no heart at all to tell her to be still for Ruthie had been born feet first, which in addition to ripping her mama apart had been the sign, as her people had always known, for one who wanders but is seldom content. Sighing, Miriam put her hand to the small of her back and felt the achy-ness of the day's troubles nudging at her.

"So whoever wants to eat must wash up now, okay. And how about someone clears the cards off the table, hmm?" Sip hastened to gather the cards and wash his hands, standing on his toes at the laundry sink in the scullery, but Ruthie shot her a *why him?* look and showed her disdain by swiping at her shorts with the backs of her hands. Ho, girl, thought Miriam, one day you'll push me too far. She dished up three plates at the stove, first arranging the steaming pap and then piling on chicken wings and thighs, and the good thick gravy. Sip set out the knives and forks, the serviette rack, the little salt and pepper set and three water glasses. Seeing these last, Ruthie finally stirred herself and ran to the fridge for the Coca-Cola, which was a Friday night treat—sometimes repeated on the weekend but Friday night always.

"So, Sipho my boy, tell me something," said Ruthie. The Coca-Cola always rendered her expansive and forgiving and now she gestured with her fork in the air. "Satisfy my curiosity. What d'you plan to do with your life, my little man?"

Sip stared at her. He didn't care for Coca-Cola but was afraid to ask for milk and he had but a vague notion of her meaning. It was always this way when she called him "Sipho, my boy" or "my little man." At these times her words seemed edged with light so that he could barely look at them. Helplessly he gazed at Miriam, who spoke to him in Zulu. "Oh," he said when she had finished, "I am growing up to be a piano player." He said this very simply and went back to eating his chicken and pap with quick, delicate movements as if he were already at the pinnacle of his profession and the simple kitchen meal divided hastily between the three and served from the pot were a state banquet.

"Indeed," said Ruthie, all eyes, "in*deed*! Well, I'll be." She was impressed despite herself for Sip's calm assurance

Nightwatching

was utterly convincing, but scorn had become habitual to her that summer and she reddened and burned under its harsh light. "Indeed," she continued, gazing at him, her head cocked, "a piano player, is that so. And not a musician, hmm? Not a pianist? A p-i-a-a-nist?"

"Tcha, stop fooling with the boy, meisie." Miriam suddenly remembered about the Coca-Cola and poured Sip a glass of milk. "And what's wrong with you today that you must be so uphill?" But Ruthie was working up a scale with her fingers on the sticky oilcloth, shrieking with laughter and trilling *la la la lala la la* over and over again in a diminishing scale to show Sip where he must place his fingers and how he must toss his head at the final crashing chord so as to be sure to catch and balance the applause on the tip of his nose, and Miriam could have smacked her, truly she could have, but presently she saw that Sip had joined in the bloody noise, giggling and drumming his fingers along the oilcloth keyboard, so she felt in her apron pocket for her tin of snuff and leaned back for a moment in her chair.

A pinch in one nostril and then the other, a count of five, and then the rolling sneezes that seemed to begin at the base of her spine and which she caught, *one two three*, in the crumpled hanky that she always kept handy in her apron pocket. Yoh weh, thought Miriam, when she'd recovered, there was nothing like a good sneeze. Ruthie and Sip were still fooling around, playing their music on the table, rattling knives and forks with their high spirits and causing the glasses to slop Coca-Cola and milk this way and that, but for once Miriam didn't mind. Shame, it was nice to see the children having fun.

"Come, Sipho my boy," Ruthie said kindly. "Let us adjourn to the conservatory and I will show you how to play 'Chopsticks.'"

The beam on Sip's face was ferocious. Swiftly he wiped his plate clean of gravy with what was left of his pap, then, with a sideways dart of his eyes in Miriam's direction, he scrambled after Ruthie. She already had the piano lid up and had flung off the old green felt lining that ran along the keys and was supposed to keep the dust away.

"Stand here," she directed Sip, pushing him into place to the right of her and making him stick out his index finger. "I'll play the melody beginning with middle C—which is this fascinating key here—and you must just keep going like this, okay?" She demonstrated, scowling with the concentration that even the most rudimentary exercise seemed to instill in her, pulling at the skin of her bottom lip with her teeth and every few seconds swiping at her fringe so that it stood up about her temples, wet and clumped.

From the kitchen Miriam heard the halting melodic line, Ruthie's hard-won demonstration piece, cut by the

Nightwatching

untroubled staccato of Sip's counterpoint. Ho, that one was a quick learner!

"Not bad, my boy," came Ruthie's voice. "A little too fast on the entry and your expression could do with improvement. Remember, music is harmony and harmony is, is—but okay, yes, on the whole."

A while later, Ruthie wandered into the kitchen looking for something to eat, something more to eat, tcha, and Miriam was just about to tell her to *shut the piano, don't you dare leave it open all night, not like last time, and that means put the green felt back on and neatly, neatly, you hear?*, when they both heard it, same thing. Miriam could tell it was a shock to Ruthie by the look on her face, which was like a bite of onion. And perhaps Miriam's face had this look too, her mouth round and open to let the surprise out, and by the time they'd settled down Sip was almost finished playing through "Chopsticks," which he'd accomplished, both parts—the rippling left-handed melody and the right handed only just-learned jab—near perfectly, as far as Miriam could tell.

"Whoa!" said Ruthie.

"Yoh weh!" Miriam couldn't help herself. She put both hands to her mouth and bit down hard upon the onion of surprise. "But where did you learn to, to—" Words failed her. From the music room came the uninterrupted babble of the contagious little tune that Miriam knew so well through all the stops and starts of Ruthie's learning of it but never played as it was now, easy and jaunty as if someone were leaning back upon his tailbone and squinting against the smoke from the cigarette that dangled from his mouth as he played. And that boy, she told herself, he's not even tall enough to reach the pedals. Wonders!

But even as she was thinking this she was reaching out to grab a handful of something that might keep Ruthie by her—the back of her shorts, her damp shirt collar—for she knew that girl and her hasty temper. Too late. *Bang* went the piano lid and then a yelp as of a puppy surprised by its owner's vengefulness. Fingers, she told herself. And she ran for the ice tray, clicking her tongue and murmuring "Tula, tula" to the boy, who was torn between pride at his undreamed-of skill and heartbreak at what this skill, almost immediately, had brought him. "Tula, tula, baba."

For a moment Miriam looked around her, thinking to admonish Ruthie, but the child was long gone.

Later, after the boy, still clutching his hand to his chest, had finished his Milo with extra sugar stirred in for the shock and she had shooed him from the kitchen, after she had stood for a moment in the driveway, her hands on her hips as she contemplated the bicycle skid marks in the gravel road, after she had calmed apprehension with a prayer for

Nightwatching

that spinning girl—may the good Lord quiet her soul and keep her safe—Miriam shrugged once, *uh*-huh. Throwing back her head she laughed heartily at something that had occurred earlier in the day and only now struck her on the funny bone. "Volume of magnitude," she repeated to herself, "a hundred times a hundred. Plural."

One thing that suited Ruthie about her father being away for the weekend the only thing perhaps but considerable—was that she could stay out as late as she liked and no one noticed. It was Miriam's habit to go to bed early, always had been. No sooner were the dishes stacked up on the drying board and the dishcloth wrung out and stretched between the kitchen faucets, no sooner was the scullery swept out and the curtains twitched shut than Miriam, yawning, would call her good-nights to the house as she turned her back on it.

But there was an element of wistfulness to Ruthie's bravado, for when had it not been a simple matter to slip out of the house at night? Miriam lived out of earshot behind the kitchen and her dad slept too soundly to be woken by his daughter's wayward comings and goings. "Like a log," he would have said, indeed had said on many occasions when the specific occasion of Ruthie's unremarked absence was not in question. All she had to do was wait patiently for the familiar log-saw of his sudden fall into sleep before letting herself out of the back door that nobody had ever thought to lock. The waiting was not always easy to accomplish but Lionel Blackburn was a man of sound habits, retiring to bed early and rising early and never thinking to check on his daughter. Why, he would as soon venture into the servant's quarters to rouse Miriam as stir himself to knock upon his daughter's bedroom door.

As for Miriam, by the end of the day weariness fell upon her as abruptly as darkness fell upon Africa. "Good night, Mr. Blackburn, good night, Ruthie," and she'd teeter, half asleep on her feet at the kitchen door. "Sleep tight."

Indeed, even on the odd nights when Mr. Blackburn was away, she'd still call good night to him. It was the habit of many years and difficult to break and perhaps it was this reflex that half convinced her that her employer was sitting at the dining room table, doing his Ledger as he did almost every night. Besides, if Ruthie were to need her Miriam, she was right there, wasn't she? Sleeping in her room in the servant's quarters behind the kitchen. But when had Ruthie last needed Miriam in the middle of the night? Sometimes this freedom from adult regard made Ruthie feel reckless and brave as if a high clear wind was blowing through her, the kind that blew across the Free State sky in autumn,

Nightwatching

turning her thoughts into windows that opened and shut. But more often she just felt melancholy.

Tonight was one of those melancholy times, Ruthie camped out in the little-kids' park with nothing better to do than scrape her tennis shoes in the dust beneath the swings. No money to spend on sweets at the Greek Caffy or chips at the fish-and-chip shop. Too early to go sliding between the shadows of the houses along Unicor Road, catching sight of the families in their lit windows as they sat at their tables eating supper or dealing cards. Too late to go home again, much too. No friends and nothing to do.

The *no friends* part was a puzzle and one she'd tried to solve many times over the last year, patiently thinking to herself, *Well, what if?* and *No*, or *maybe—*, and then, towards the end, *So what? Big bloody deal!* The truth was she had no clear idea why the kids at Weltevreden Primary had taken against her, gradually at first and then less so, until it was just Trudy Mason and her sitting against the netball post at break, and then there'd been the terrible falling-out with Trudy, who'd been welcomed back—gladly, it seemed—by their old circle, and Ruthie was left all by herself, entirely alone. And rather than dawdle at the edges of the playground, a regular Charlie and fooling no one, Ruthie had taken to spending all her free time at the school library, which, if it wasn't exactly a pleasure, was at least beneath the notice of everyone else, and it was here, slumped at a rickety school desk with the names of ten generations of bored schoolchildren incised upon its surface, that she was discovering how to disappear between the pages of a book so that anyone—a teacher, a prefect, a library monitor—popping their heads in at the little prefab building that housed the idiosyncratic collection of largely donated picture books and adult mysteries and adventure serials would see no one, no one at all, and go away appeased.

Miss Priestly, the librarian, was a horror. A lumpy-sweatered, tightly permed creature who wouldn't let food near her books, so that unless Ruthie went around the back of the prefab to wolf down the cheese and apricot jam sandwiches that Miriam always packed for her lunch she went hungry. What horrified Ruthie most about Miss Priestly wasn't the lumpy sweaters or the terrible clenched hair or even the harsh rules she'd laid down to do with the separation of books and food. Miss Priestly had done a much worse thing. Once, long ago, she'd been kind to Ruthie, and the sour taint of her breath as she bent down to ask the girl what books she liked to read—"What kind of story, my girl?"—lingered still. Halfway through last term the librarian had turned white as a ghost, then yellow, then left the school abruptly and the rumour was that she was on sick leave and deathly ill. Dead by now, Ruthie hoped, and in her grave.

Nightwatching

Mrs. Bentley, the substitute librarian, was always on the phone to her daughter in Johannesburg and although the ruling about food and books still held firm in theory, in practice it was a mere sleight-of-hand for Ruthie to lounge at her desk, her head buried in last year's *Guinness Book of World Records*, unwrapping the cheese and jam sandwiches in their waxed paper under cover of Mrs. Bentley's exclamations over the delighted exploits of this or that sainted grandchild. Nineteen seventy-five had been a year packed with men who ate razor blades and bicycle parts and hot dogs in record time.

The library was wonderfully cool in summer but freezing in winter. "Them's the breaks, kid," as her father would say, affecting an American accent.

Ruthie had been bent almost double, thinking and dragging her tennis shoes through the dust. The iron links of the swing clanged against the A-bar as she straightened out and looked around. The park was hardly ever empty, not entirely, and even now she could see two older boys leaning against the monkey bars in the far corner. They were smoking and fooling around, their voices travelling easily towards her across the dusk. "No, man, she's a dog—" "I'm telling you . . . in like Flynn . . ." One began to jostle the other but it was just rough play, Ruthie could tell, nothing meant but the affection boys couldn't show each other anyway else. Nor anyone else, Ruthie sometimes thought. Two summers ago her father had stopped kissing her good night, just stopped for no reason she could tell, and a dark space the size of the world had opened in her. He'd never been a hugger, not ever, so that was one thing she didn't miss. If things were different anyplace else, Ruthie didn't know about it. All she'd ever been was here.

One of the boys pushed the other away from the monkey bars and began running in a wide curve across the park. His friend gave chase. Soon they'd pass Ruthie on her swing; she knew she was beneath their notice, although she longed to beg a cigarette off the good-looking one. She was trying to teach herself to smoke; it would be good practice for the glamorous life she planned to lead one day and meanwhile might help to stunt her growth, which was getting to be entirely out of control if feet and hands were anything to go by.

"Why, you are a regular Labrador," her father had exclaimed the last time she complained that her sandals were too small, so now she just went around in her tennis shoes, which was fine anyway for stealth, or barefoot, which was cool at least. He hadn't meant to hurt her feelings, he just spoke plainly and without breaking any teeth over his words.

Suddenly the good-looking one, the one with a tan and floppy blond hair, caught sight of her. "Hey, check it out." He gestured to his mate, at the same time letting out a sound she'd sometimes heard before when the high school boys walked past a girl. It was a sort of hiss made from the top of the mouth and through clenched teeth—*kisskk kisskk kisskk*—the sound you'd use to call a cat indoors. Now the other boy turned and stared right at Ruthie and as he walked towards her he made the sound again, *kisskk kisskk kisskk*.

"Hey, cut that out—" Ruthie tried to form the words, failed, and decided instead that she'd just ignore him in a dignified yet fascinating way. Sometimes when boys made that sound to certain girls, loose girls, girls who peeled their school socks way down below their ankle bones and who yanked their gymslips high above their knees and who hung around the bicycle sheds at break with smoke on their breath and ragged, rebellious fingernails, those girls would laugh and toss their hair and yell back funny-rude things to the boys that would make them titter and squirm and dig their hands hard into their pockets. But next day they'd be back for more.

"*Kisskk kisskk kisskk*, here, pussy."

A really terrible blush began in Ruthie's armpits and travelled rapidly all the way up her chest, over her throat, across the whole surface of her face and into her hairline. She could feel it spread, not evenly but in blotches, for she had studied herself in the bathroom mirror once or twice during similar but private paroxysms and knew the spectacle to be an ugly one. The cheeks would be glowing disks of humiliation, the forehead a shiny beacon of distress blinking on and off, and the throat mottled and patchy. Oh no, she thought, oh no oh no oh no. She closed her eyes and imagined herself, a red girl throbbing dully from her crimson toes to the top of her scarlet head. It was always the way, always. The slightest thing could set her off: a chance remark from one of the commercial travellers, the teacher calling on her to recite "Ozymandias" in class, her father's sarcasm. And now this, this dimly understood alliance between cats and girls which she perceived to be at once more witty, more dangerous, more charged with forbidden meaning than she would ever grasp. But she understood none of it.

Mutely she hung her head and suffered.

When she opened her eyes again the park was empty, the boys presumably intent upon their wayward, elsewhere lives. Nearly empty. Here and there dark figures moved in the shadows, black folks stretching their legs before returning to their small rooms behind the kitchens of other people's houses. She got off the swing and passed a couple of women still wearing their overalls, but the men handing around a brown-paper-wrapped bottle beneath the eucalyptus trees were already changed out of their work clothes. They looked up as she walked by but without curiosity; she was nothing to them. The world was an echoing place at these times, vast and star-filled, and there was no one in all the night to say, *Go home, girl, run along, do.*

It was at such times, the park bulging a little with the day's measure of despondency, that Ruthie would remember the terrible thing that Trudy Mason had called her. It was in the context of the lunch sandwiches that Miriam packed for Ruthie every day and which were always apricot jam and cheese filling, always, but where was the harm in that? Why should a girl not have apricot jam and cheese sandwiches for her lunch *every day of the year* if that's where her heart lay? Miriam, when applied to, merely shrugged, "But you like cheese and jam, meisie, always have."

"Poor motherless girl," Trudy Mason had said, putting her arm about Ruthie's shoulders. *Trying* to put her arm, rather, for that arm never reached its destination. Not even close. Instead it was grabbed and yanked and pinched. Twisted, even.

"Ruthven! Ruthven! What in God's name—" Mrs. Bakkes had come running and some of the other teachers, but it was too late. The other girls had already turned from her, taking the sobbing Trudy with them. What had she done but offer the motherless girl a hug? That Ruthie was motherless was without question—their own mothers had declared it—that she was vicious was now demonstrable.

With an effort of will, Ruthie turned her thoughts away

from the incident that had cost her so dear. She'd spend the rest of the summer in the park if she had to or rattling about on her bike or flung up against the windows of other people's lives but she was not in the mood for pity, *no siree*.

With this last indignant thought, she threw herself once more onto her bicycle and began to pedal across the back lane that would take her over to the next street but one. There was a house she was interested in on Bleeker Street. It had been vacant for three months, ever since old man Harris died, but recently a large red Sold sign had indicated the return of life and only last week a moving van had been drawn up to the curb all of one morning while a couple of men in denim boiler suits lunged up and down the driveway, sweating and swearing and yelling instructions to one another. Ruthie had held off her inspection until she could be certain that the homeowners, whoever they might be, were properly settled in. She always waited until the curtains were up, anyway. Of course some people might think that the best time to look in on a new family was right at the beginning, but Ruthie was too experienced a watcher to make that mistake again.

For a newly moved family was a nervous thing, catlike and twitchy. The open boxes that stood around, the makeshift meals cooling on the kitchen table, the children rubbing at their eyes and waiting for their sheets to be dug up out of mislaid crates; all these events turned parents cranky, made them peer out into the night with spiteful eyes. Twice she'd been spotted, and the second time the father, a burly fellow, a mine boss on transfer, had lurched from the house yelling blue murder—you'd have thought she was a tsotsi. He'd almost caught her, and would have too, except for the adjustment his eyes had had to make between light and darkness, and while he'd staggered about on the back stairs shaking his head and bellowing she'd ducked under his arms and run hell for leather.

Ruthie's eyes were naturally trained to the dark, always had been.

But, once the curtains were up, the family seemed to relax a little. It was as if the curtains going up were the signal to let their guard down, collectively and all at once. Now a watcher might ride her bike all the way up to the garden gate, climb around to the back and take stock. If there was a bush close by to sit beneath, that would do, or a handy tree with thick foliage, but sometimes there was nothing for it but to make one's way in a sort of Indian crawl to the side of the house where one could crouch beneath the eaves. At times like this Ruthie would press her whole body against the brickwork, still warm from the heat of the day, and wait for her heart to stop skittering about in her chest like a crazy animal. There was no way to make her heart quieten, she knew; she aimed just to cage apprehension. Then she would inch herself up to the pane of glass, to the window that was cool against her hot forehead. Sometimes there were burglar bars, arabesques and curls, but more often not. The front rooms that faced the street had stiff lace curtains but the back rooms had sun filters and these were occasionally not quite closed by the maids whose job it was to whisk them open first thing in the morning when they came in early to make the tea and shut them again in the evening, moving through the houses briskly or wearily or sadly or contrarily, the sun going down but their working day not yet over.

Ruthie had been a watcher of one sort or another for as long as she could remember. When she was very young she would hide under the dining room table while her dad played poker with the commercial travellers, hugging her legs to her chest and sucking the salt from her knees. Or she would sit very still in a corner of the room while he did his accounts, pretending to read her *Beano Annual* but keeping an eye on him as he marked down columns of figures in the hardcover exercise book in which he had written the names of every one of the boys who worked for him at the store: Lucas, Wilson, Clanwilliam, Jonas, Themba. At other times she sneaked into the kitchen and skulked about in the pantry listening to Miriam as she clattered about amongst the pots and pans, leaving the kitchen door open and calling out to this one or that one as they walked past,

"Shew, Lindiwe, it's hot, my baby!"

"Dumela, Snoekie, any post for the baas?"

"Hey, Annie, have you seen that terrible child who lives here? Ugly thing?"

So, Miriam had known all along about Ruthie hiding beneath the stone laundry sink in the scullery. It made Ruthie crazy to think that she couldn't fool Miriam, hadn't yet anyway. Bloody. After that Ruthie took her watching elsewhere, right out of the house at least. She was afraid of Miriam's hilarity and besides there was nothing to discover in the house she'd grown up in. Her body responded to the old house seemingly without her volition, her legs beginning to fly when they reached the hallway with its thin runner of faded rosettes that she leapt over and her hands reaching out to touch her bedroom walls with their familiar tilt and worn-smooth places where she rested her arms above her bed. The concrete step was cool against her feet in summer and the smell of furniture polish in the music room made her sneeze every second Tuesday. There were flypapers hanging in the kitchen and dining room and pantry and at night Miriam lit mosquito coils that burnt with an acrid smell that rubbed off on her hands and face.

Might as well take her watching elsewhere, and so she

did. First to the music teacher's back garden, where she learned stillness by sitting for hours under the privet hedge, listening to snatches of program from the radio and watching the beginning of a shadow darken every hour or so in the corner of a window. Then lighten again. The wind shook and rattled the stars in the high, clear platteland sky. Harder towards midnight. Ruthie was learning stillness but boredom ambushed her in the guise of curiosity. Tomorrow she would venture farther afield, creep closer to the window, press her eager face to the transparent glass of other people's lives. She climbed out from beneath her bush and the privet barely rustled.

After that it just became a habit, more so in the summer and most of all on weekends when her dad was out of town and restlessness drove her to flop about from one room to another all day, satisfied with nothing, hungry all right though food made no difference. Thirsty too, thank the Lord for Coca-Cola. Only thing loosened the throat's slow noose. "Whoa, girl," Miriam would say, "get out from between my feet. Read a book, why don't you, or practise your piano. Piano could do with a little practice, piano's getting dusty and so are you, tcha!" But Ruthie was exhausted from her night's wanderings and when she picked up a book would run the same sentence over and over in her mind like a strand of music picked out with one finger—neither made any sense.

This summer was different though, or maybe not. No different in the wandering, the silent watching, the snatches of radio music from open windows at night, the itchy stillness beneath bushes, the cool glass against her face and the day's stored warmth of bricks against her body, the pins and needles shaken out of her limbs, the stars revolving in great wheels through the heavens, moons waxing and waning, the hasty cycle home through the strange and familiar darkness of neighbourhood streets. Why different then? Ruthie would have been hard pressed to say. Something had come loose in her for one thing, a connection. Now she was unanchored, a fidgety creature with no ease or hope of it to come. Her clothes were too small, her hands and feet too large. She woke up with salt on her cheeks although she could never remember her dreams or even the event of them. At odd moments of the day words would fly into her head and lodge there and she would whisper them over and over without knowing what they fully meant—*I wish . . . I want . . . I will . . .* Sometimes minutes would pass in this way before she became aware of the words and then the world would rush back into her body and she'd catch herself and think, *But what, what do I want?* There was no satisfactory answer, just the asking and how this asking persisted through minutes at a time—the sun moving across a patch of grass, the wind rising and falling, a sudden soaking afternoon rain shower—

and still she would sit there staring vacantly into space, the words blowing through her, *I wish . . . I want . . . I will . . .*

Some days she loved the world and everyone in it with a passionate love, her heart too full for her chest, kindness moving her to tears. On days like this everything made her happy, the hard blue sky, the scud of a sunbeam in the music room, the rumble of motor traffic on the macadam road. Everything: she breathed in and out with the wind, sunlight eased her edges, and if it rained why that was a blessing too and caused the grass to grow. Miriam was the best friend a girl could ever have and her daddy was simply the greatest. She would have lavished him with kisses if he'd let her; as it was she contented herself with seeing to his clothes: setting out his jacket on its night hanger and brushing it down in the morning, polishing up his shoes to a high gloss and laying them down on a square of newspaper in front of the washing machine. And she would arrange his pigskin toiletry kit on his dresser in the morning, the silver-backed brushes, the safety razor and shaving brush with its fat tuft of soft bristles. There.

But at other times—ah, here was the strange part—a black rushing sickness of the soul would consume her and then it was as if the sky had gone dark and whirling cinders obscured the sun. Everything hurt her: the clatter of breakfast dishes in the sink and Miriam's back turned away from her, the roar of the toast as her father briskly scraped butter back and forth, the dryness of the earth between the aloes that lined the driveway. The world pressed up against her and the world was no longer inanimate, a place in which to live, but a living thing, a poking snouted creature with a thousand prodding knees, and elbows that flew and jerked. Oh, how it hurt her, this world with its sharp edges and magnificent cruelties. The dog run over in the street and the faded colours of the awnings on Main Street and the weary queues of workers lined up at the bus depot and the lonely shift whistle that sounded away on the mines. *I wish . . . I want . . . I will . . .* but there was no ease to be had in reverie and no answer to be found in idle questioning.

The house on Bleeker Street looked dark amongst the other lit houses on the block, like a sudden gap in a full set of teeth, but Ruthie decided to go on around the back and try her luck anyway. And when she'd flattened her bike under the bushes and crept about the side of the small brick house she was glad she had, because there was a light on in a downstairs room and the window was covered by thin lace curtains, the flimsy kind same as the Harrises had, in fact, now that she looked closely, exactly the same. Mrs. Harris must have just left them there when old man Harris died and the new owners hadn't had a chance to take them down yet. Ho, some people! Ruthie rolled her eyes to the heavens and made a silent little tutting sound to herself because she just didn't understand grown-ups and their ways and their tolerance for dusty swags of lace. Other people's too, well!

But it was as easy to see through the thin lace curtains into the new people's house as it had been easy to see into the Harrises' living room and Ruthie noted at once that the light was not the flickering blue sort that was the very best kind of light there was. Television had come to the country earlier that year and now even people in small towns like Welkom could watch broadcasts for a couple of hours in the evening. On her travels Ruthie saw them, these lucky few families, but more and more lately, sitting in tight semicircles with their eyes intent on the aquatic light that seemed to bubble up from the depths of these boxes. Even when the evening broadcast was over, the continuity announcer taking his leave in English or Afrikaans, the family would sit there for a moment, dazed, their eyes still fixed hopefully on the brightly coloured but unmoving test pattern.

With all her heart Ruthie yearned for a television set but her father was not a man for newfangled devices. He was content with the daily newspaper that he read patiently and over the course of the entire day, from front to back cover, and with the radio that he still called the wireless. "Let's see if it proves itself, my girl," he told Ruthie, and he was consequently deaf to her pleas and her wheedling and her increasingly high-strung arguments that the rest of the world, *the rest of the world*, had been watching television for twenty years, had they not, and were they living in the dark ages here in this rotten dump at the forsaken bottom of Africa? Well, were they? "Let's just wait and see, my girl," said her father, wearing her out with his implacable vegetable patience.

So, no television, and the Harrises hadn't had one either. Bloody. It wasn't as if Ruthie could see much from outside the window anyway, just colours sometimes and movements if they were large enough. Faces, occasionally. But the flickering blue light was its own talisman; it was the cold fire before which she warmed her lonesome heart. If she stared at it long enough from behind the various neighbourhood windowpanes Ruthie would feel herself go into a trance and some part of her cold and nervous soul would be eased. Then Ruthie herself would cease to be, just for a moment, the moth girl that fluttered forever against the windows of other people's brightly illuminated lives.

Ruthie kept her cheeks between her knees for a while and breathed in the smell of herself. When she was calm again she climbed from beneath her bush and tiptoed around the side of the house and retrieved her bike. It wasn't late yet, not very late, and she pondered her choices. The Van Onselens down the street always listened to *Squad Cars* on the radio on a Friday night with the sound turned up loudly to accommodate Oupa, and she wasn't averse to joining them as she sometimes did, lolling in the comfy shrubbery beneath the open summer room, but Friday night was also the night the Benders, just four blocks over on Delmont Road, did their sex. Tracey and Gavin Bender had been trying to have a baby for the last year, according to Dolly, the Benders' maid. Ruthie had heard Miriam and Dolly exclaiming over this, shaking their heads and clicking their tongues. A year was a long time to try to have a baby and Ruthie was hoping that all the sex would help.

Well, perhaps? she thought, and then, *Why not?* The moon was a funny old thing, a ball some kid had tossed so high it hadn't come down yet, and it would give her no trouble as she lay in the tall grass beneath the Benders' bedroom window. The grass was always nice and thick on Friday night because Saturday morning was Mr. Bender's morning for mowing the lawn. He was regular as clockwork, Mr. Bender, you could set your watch by him. Friday night he did his sex and Saturday morning he cut his grass.

But when she got to Delmont Road she could already see that something was different because the garden of number 34 was lousy with coloured fairy lights strung through the trees and all the electric lights in the house were on and none of the curtains were drawn so anyone passing by outside could observe the party going on inside. It looked like they were having a high old time. Ruthie could see folks holding drinks and others dancing to records in the living room. A maid in a starched apron was walking around with food on a tray.

So, thought Ruthie, perhaps they've decided not to have that baby after all. She hunkered down in a bush beside the swimming pool out back trying to decide if this was a good thing or a bad thing and decided that, on the whole, it was a very good thing because, one, babies were dumb, two, they were a noise and a nuisance and, three, if Mrs. Bender swelled up like a pumpkin with a baby inside her there was a very good chance that Mr. Bender wouldn't love her anymore, or worse he would still love her and then she would die while the baby was trying to get born. It had happened before and even to her own dad.

But on the other hand, my girl, she puffed her cheeks out in imitation of Mr. Feinstein, her father's partner, who prided himself on his fair-mindedness and was always juggling hands in an argument, so much so, her dad would complain, that he was less than useless when it came to ordering stock or settling a dispute amongst the boys at the Concession Store. On the *other* hand, some people seemed to like babies. Some people seemed to *really* like them. For instance, all the maids in the neighbourhood would bring their babies to Miriam and she'd press her face into their stomachs and blow until their arms and legs would jerk about and they'd shriek with laughter. Miriam would laugh too, and the mothers, until it was a bloody circus out there in the backyard. No, on the whole, Ruthie thought, it was probably a good idea to forget about the baby and have a party instead.

The party itself was spilling out into the garden with men and women carrying drinks and cigarettes and little party serviettes drifting towards the swimming pool. Cautiously Ruthie looked out from her bush but the noise and the music and the snippets of grown-up conversation were at once so loud and so alien that she felt cloaked in invisibility, free to watch and listen without fear of discovery. "I tell you frankly—" "Well, if that's her attitude why don't you—" "Nee wat, man, what's a girl to do?" Someone had turned the music up inside the house and a couple began to jig about on the Slasto edging the pool. Others clustered around egging them on: "Don't fall in, hey!" and "Hold her tighter, you Charlie!" and so on. Soon others joined the first two, swaying loosely to the tinny music and laughing with the hard blunted laughter adults used to show off their enjoyment.

Well, if that doesn't take the cake, Ruthie thought to herself, blowing out her cheeks once more. She had meant to be fascinated by the party because the life to come, she was certain, would be full of parties, but now she was not so sure. At night in her narrow child's bed, unable to sleep for the ache in her legs and the fretful solitary ache in her heart that was not like a growing pain because it had been with her always, she calmed restlessness with imagination. At these times she pictured herself in Paris and New York and Cairo, and in these glittering cities of the mind she wore filmy white evening dresses with shoulder straps and silver sandals and drifted from one cocktail party to the next. Imagination was her oldest, and this summer her only, friend.

By now someone had fallen into the swimming pool and someone else had jumped in to "save" her and was fooling around splashing water at the other guests, and most of the women were giggling and making a terrible noise and the men were yelling to beat the band and trying to push each other in. Ruthie heard the retch and spatter of a man being sick in a bush nearby. "Jislaaik!" he muttered, then he groaned once and vomited again. She put her fingers in her ears to block out the sound and when she took them out again she heard a man's voice on the other side of her and he was saying quickly but over and over again, "No please come on please no please come on please . . ." And this over and over and quicker and quicker with great ragged pants between and a woman was squealing, *like a stuck pig* her dad would have said, but it gave Ruthie a queer feeling to think of her father now.

Cautiously she poked her head out and peered into the

darkness behind the pool house where the sound was coming from. At first she saw nothing but gradually her eyes adjusted to the dimness and she made out—but what was it?—a man, yes, it was a man leapfrogging a woman but stuck halfway. Bare-bottomed, hairy-bummed, his trousers caught about his ankles, he was struggling to get loose but each lunge seemed to hurt the woman, who squealed on and on into the night.

Once again Ruthie put her fingers in her ears and this time she crouched down very low and stayed that way for a long time. She tried not to think of anything at all but this proved to be impossible so she began to recite "Ozymandias" to herself. Last term Mrs. Bakkes had made the kids memorize "Ozymandias" and one by one they'd had to stand at the front of the class and recite the poem with extra marks for expression. Memory work, it was called, and very important for discipline of mind, Mrs. Bakkes said. The order was alphabetical so Ruthie was second and she'd gotten full marks for memory but almost nothing for expression since the only way she'd trained herself to memorize the poem was in one great spurt, no breaths between lines, no pauses for understanding. But the words to "Ozymandias," their lift and fall, the glad cadence of their half-rhyme, were curiously reassuring, and although Ruthie had but the vaguest notion of the poem's meaning she had taken to whispering

Nightwatching

it to herself over and over whenever she was bewildered or anxious or otherwise suffering in whatever nameless yet painful way that the summer had chosen to inflict upon her. Now she took a deep breath and began: "I met a traveller fromanantiqueland who said twovastandtrunklesslegsofstone stand in the desert."

After a while she felt, as she always did, lulled, as if the long unbroken lines were drifts of sand running through her hands in some dreamy rocking Sahara of the mind.

In her white nightgown with its bit of blue eyelet lace about the throat, the music teacher looked uncommonly handsome as she leaned out of her bedroom window. It was a shame that there was no one to observe her in this interesting state of heightened beauty. Except for the moon, she mourned, but she was accustomed to such setbacks. She bent one rounded arm and watched her lacy sleeve bell away in graceful folds, then propped her chin on her palm.

"Oh, thank you, Mr. Blackburn," she whispered, for in her imagination her handsome neighbour had stooped to light the cigarette she held between her fingers. Indeed, this cigarette and the business of its lighting, its elegant exhaling of smoke and the necessity for this smoke to be blown past the net curtains and out the window, was one of the reasons that Bettina Foley was leaning, like an old-fashioned heroine, in the moonlight. The other reason was more complicated and had to do with Mr. Blackburn's recalcitrant daughter, Ruthie, whom Bettina had long suspected of night wandering. Now, she tossed her braid over her shoulder and exhaled deeply. The smoke drifted out into the air in a ragged ring and hung there for a moment before dispersing on a breeze that was at once too small and too weak to be discerned by the woman in her stuffy little house.

She was about to bang down her casement with an expression of disgust when she heard the sound of bicycle wheels whirring along the service road. There was no doubt in her mind that it was the terrible unmusical child returning home from God alone knew what mischief, but to make certain, Bettina was obliged to lean out as far as she could and peer into the darkness until Ruthie's characteristic slumped outline was apparent as she edged swiftly towards the side door.

Oh, was there ever such a loveless creature! thought the music teacher, by which she meant, had anyone been curious enough to inquire, a girl incapable of love, as well as the more generally accepted notion—a creature whom others deemed unlovable.

Nightwatching

It was quite true that Miriam loved babies. She'd had three of her own—loved them all. She loved their fat warm stomachs that hummed like engines and the dimpled flesh above their elbows and knees. She loved the sweet powderish smell that hovered above their heads like halos and their wet fat mouths whether these mouths were curled in sleep or open in endless baby rage. Oh, and toes! Oh, and fingers! She loved to turn them over and sling them in a blanket across her back and feel the warmth of them all day, little legs hanging down over her ribs. "Tula, baba," sleep my baby, she'd murmur to Jericho, Jonas and later their little sister, Temperance Thandile, whose birth she had so longed for but whose nature was so far from temperate that Temper it had straight away become and Temper it had stuck, although her fond mama still called her Thandile in the hope that she would one day outgrow her childish and wilful ways.

All the domestics loved babies, it only made sense, since a domestic was allowed to keep her baby with her but when the child was weaned he must go straight away to live with the grandmother out by the Location on the outskirts of town. In these circumstances it was better to love a baby a little more and a child a little less. But even so, the love that Miriam had for babies was special; she was famous for it. All the maids in the neighbourhood brought their newborns to her and she would heft them in her arms and assess their weight within an ounce. "Tcha, this one is a good sleeper, is he not? And you, my little baba, are you hungry already?" And she would assist an anxious new mother with her breastfeeding or advise a young wife on how to keep her husband satisfied when he came home on his monthly visit from the mines to find a small downy head on the pillow beside her.

Yes, Miriam loved babies, but about other matters she was pragmatic and wholly without illusions. For the life of her people shamed her and brought her daily to her knees where she suffered, silently it is true—few would have discerned that beneath the domestic overall and apron beat such a rebellious heart and yet such a quiet one too—but suffered, yes, on and on. Her people, how they shamed her! But it wasn't their fault. How many years of suffering had passed and of such intensity; how many men had called the white man baas and master? How many women had shrugged off their own children in order to carry white children on their backs, then tend these same children and, yes, even grow to love them? Love! Was this the final betrayal? Sighing, Miriam tightened the knot at the back of her doek as if drawing the two sides of her argument to a close. Yes, love.

Well, and then? In this very town the shift whistles blew and black men marched into the mines as if they were marching into war, but the earth was implacable. She turned over, she trapped men inside her, she exploded without warning and lives, many lives, were lost. The white bosses stayed up late to talk to the news and shake their heads—*what a pity, too bad, such a terrible waste.* But what of the families left behind when the wage earners were killed? What of the widows and orphaned children, what of the hunger and hardship that was their only legacy? In this very town a woman might find herself working for a white family that abused her but whether or not the very worst happened—a beating or a rape—it was certain that this woman would be demeaned in all the small and spiteful kitchen ways that only she would feel and having felt them must swallow and turn her attention to another task as if to say, *I am not here, I do not signify.* Thus if the white madam locked up the sugar and the jam so her maid could not steal from her, if she was only allowed two weeks at Christmas to go home and see her children, and if on returning her madam took one look at her and said, "Well, my girl, I hope you will not try to tell me you are in the family way again," what could this woman do but shrug and blow the air from her cheeks. She was not a woman, she was a maid. At times like this it seemed to Miriam that the long hard history of her people would come crashing down on her shoulders, and she'd lay her head down on her arms at the kitchen table and remain that way while the little red clock ticked like a pulse above her head.

Do? What could she do? She told herself that she was luckier than most.

Not because the Blackburn family had always been good to her or because Lionel Blackburn paid her a fair wage and treated her with decorum. And not because she had a fondness for Ruthie who was a motherless child with a restless, sore heart, but tough. (Better be tough, girl, she thought, better be.) No, such things were her due; she had earned and paid for them. Why then? Her sons for one thing, her sons almost entirely.

Jericho and Jonas: they were her pride and joy. To look at them one would not think that together they balanced such a weight of knowledge between them. Jericho was slenderly built, and although Jonas had not the advantage of his brother's height he was robust and solid with sturdy shoulders as of one who always invites more weight. It was the weight of responsibility; it was the weight of his people's history. "We must work harder, my brothers"—this was his favourite phrase and one that he offered in order to solve every problem that came his way.

"More weight," his brother tutted impatiently, "well, but you are not a horse. Not yet, my brother."

Despite these differences in temperament, both her boys

had taken to schooling with such facility that Jericho had lately earned his teaching diploma and now taught history at the township primary school and Jonas was learning to be a bookkeeper at Mr. Blackburn's Concession Store on the mines. Their father had been a miner with barely a Standard Five reading level, but the conviction of his people's oppression had been as a glowing coal in his chest. It gave him no ease. And there were others on the mines eager to plot and plan, to give words to the steady, banked anger that flared so rarely. Every two months Albert Tsomela would come home on leave and then he would sit down on the floor between his sons and talk to them quietly but with great seriousness. When Jericho was seven years and Jonas five years old their father died in a mining accident, but Miriam had a good job and the little family had soldiered on.

It was quiet in the kitchen, Sunday afternoon quiet, even the flies too fat and heavy with sweetness to move. The ceiling fan gave a wobbly little clatter every now and then, the kitchen clock plucked minutes out of the air one by one, but that was all. Should she iron? No, too hot. But there was ironing to do. And supper would have to be cold as well since it was much too hot to set the oven, much too. Mr. Blackburn would be tired by the time he drove back from Bloemfontein, and hungry perhaps. Cold meats and potato salad for supper then, on rye bread. No, wait, coleslaw, that way she didn't even have to boil the potatoes. *Uh*-huh. There was the sound of water snickering in the outside drains and Sip darted into the kitchen. His feet were bare as they had been all summer and he wore an old T-shirt that she seemed to remember Ruthie had thrown out because of a rip in the sleeve. The tear had been carefully darned and the T-shirt was clean as all Sip's clothes were clean.

"Is the baas here yet?" asked Sip, running to look in the pantry.

"Tcha, and how many times have I told you his name? Mister Blackburn. Not baas, not master. Mister. Mister Blackburn."

But Sip was running from the pantry to the fridge, peering first in one and then in the other, clicking his tongue and hauling the bottles of Coca-Cola out of the plastic crate where they were stored and arranging them with great ceremony in the fridge. His eyes had the bright curious expression of a small animal and as he worked he turned his head this way and that, admiring the slight *ting* of the glass bottles as they knocked against each other, taking care not to shake them up as he lifted them from their crate and pushed them carefully to the back of the fridge. Lining them up in rows as if they were skittles. There. At last, this chore completed to his satisfaction, Sip banged the door of the refrigerator to and went to sit at the kitchen table. "All ready for Mister," he remarked to Miriam.

The more time Sip spent in the lazy bustle of the Blackburn kitchen, the more chores he took upon himself. He was a sober, responsible little fellow and seemed to feel the need to bestow his childish labour in exchange for the inert warmth offered by Miriam and Ruthie. At times his zeal discomforted Miriam; at other times she wished he would galvanize Ruthie with his industry. Now Miriam observed how he had lately claimed Coca-Cola duty, which, given Mr. Blackburn's prodigious thirst and unnatural fondness for the stuff, was a full-time job. Five, six bottles he could down daily and that wasn't even counting the time he put in at the store where, she happened to know, he kept a little bar fridge full of rattling bottles supplied by the corner caffy.

Sip had taken out his material scraps and was busying himself with his cutting. He was fashioning a summer wardrobe for Annabel and in this as in everything he attempted he was gravely professional. First he'd sketch the clothes he envisioned on pieces of newspaper, then he would pin the newspaper to his scraps. Kneeling on the floor in a corner of the kitchen, he was engaged in cutting out a little frock—it looked like?—with a pair of secateurs he'd likely secured from his father's gardening supply shed and certainly without his father's permission. He worked carefully but confidently, his fingers pinching at and straightening the bright blue satin. As always, at these times, the Barbie doll called Annabel overlooked his labours. He had rescued her at the beginning of the summer from the garbage where Ruthie had thrown her in a fit of pique and all that he did he did for her, her calm, painted gaze seeming to justify his painstaking attention.

"Whew, hot hot hot," said Miriam wiping off her forehead with the back of her arm. And then, "Is Daddy sleeping?"

Sip shrugged. It was often hard to tell with his father where sleeping began again after drunken ended and he was a particularly literal-minded boy. So shrugged. "Where is she?" he asked cautiously. But he neither expected nor received an answer. Who knew? She was a law unto herself, as Miriam would say, banging the sides of the mixing bowl hard to shake down the flour or snapping a sugar pea in half. Ho, that one! But there was something Miriam had been meaning to ask him so now she turned to where Sip sat bent over his sewing, his fingers busy, his eyes half squinched shut as if what he was seeing was all inside him, the blue satin frock of his imagination cut out against his mind's eye.

"Now that piano, my boy, that 'Chopsticks' . . . You're telling me you never heard it before?"

"No, not . . . only when she played it. She played the 'Chopsticks' through twice, but. At least."

Nightwatching

"So, how?"

"Well, she played it through. Maybe even three times, now that I'm thinking."

"But if you've never—"

Sip sighed. It was true that he'd never played on the piano, though he'd often wanted to. And sometimes he'd passed the music teacher's house and heard piano music coming from her open window. And he'd sat in this very kitchen, of course, and listened to the runs and jagged stops of Ruthie's practices (and the lid banging shut when she'd had enough and the screen door swinging on its hinges). But it was only when he'd stood beside her and watched her finger jabbing out the counterpoint and then watched again, as with the other hand she thumped out the melody, that the music seemed to pulse through his body and out his fingertips. He didn't know how to say it though, or describe the feeling that the music opened in him. Everything in him was broken in pieces and music made him whole. And then at other times music itself broke him apart; he was nothing at the end of it and could barely remember his name. This was not "Chopsticks," of course, but real music, the late-night jazz on his father's radio, the trumpet solos that seemed as lonely as the voice of the night itself, the supple clarity of a horn or an oboe.

Once he had loitered outside the music teacher's house

because he'd heard gramophone music coming from inside. The music was orchestral and stately at first but later the saddest thing he'd ever heard and later still lively as dancing and then the stately part again. But the music, or at least the listening to it, hadn't ended well because the music teacher had seen him in her garden and leaned out the window yelling, "Hey, picannin, get out this bloody minute, right now, before I call the police on you!" So that was that.

But he did not know what to tell Miriam about how he'd been able to play "Chopsticks"; he just did not know.

Miriam was grating carrots and gazing out the kitchen window. She'd forgotten the question or else forgotten the agitation that gave rise to it. She turned and watched Sip for a moment, his heavy head on its thin child's neck. Tcha! His fingers flew over the cheap satin, tucking and pulling at it, then every minute or so he would sit back on his haunches and gaze at his handiwork with his head cocked at an angle.

"Well, my son," she began kindly, "and when do you begin at Thabong Primary?" Thabong Primary was the school at which Jericho taught; he was a Standard Four teacher, the best there was.

Sip cut a thread off with his teeth and looked at her blankly. "It's important to go to school, my boy," she began again, determined to speak patiently for she'd had this discussion many times already, many times, with various chil-

Nightwatching

dren—and parents: the mothers who brought their babies to her and the mine workers who couldn't read or write and with the wrong-headedness of certain foolish men scorned that their children should learn to read and write and so outwit their prideful fathers. Miriam's heart failed her at these times but she always rallied herself for there was so much to be won and so much to be lost, and what was lost would be lost for a very long time, perhaps forever.

"Well, and who will be your teacher, do you know yet?"

Sip looked at her. He did not know how to say that his father did not, he did not . . . Anxiously he bit at the ragged cuticle of his thumbnail. Bit down hard. Then he thought of something and became loquacious with relief.

"I am not going to be attending Thabong Primary School. No, it is sad but that is all there is to it. Well, you see my father thinks, he thinks it will be a waste because of my great talent. But I'm to study for a while here in the city and then I'm to be, to become a piano player."

As he spoke Sip nodded to himself at first slowly and then more rapidly as if with each word he felt himself growing into the truth of his passionate vision. "And then after I am a great piano player I'll travel all over the world, to Johannesburg and Durban and Maseru, to the casino in Maseru especially, and I'll play the piano all the time and the people will say, 'Whoa, fella, we have never heard such playing, but never!' That is how I'll make my money and the king of Maseru will give me a big house, perhaps even with a swimming pool, but still I will come home in the end to my father and to you, Miriam, and for my father I'll bring a Mercedes-Benz, sports model, and for you a fur coat and for her, for her . . ." But there was nothing, no gift singular enough for Ruthie, his crush, his love, and Sip remained stricken, chewing distractedly at his cuticles.

Ai kona! thought Miriam and the great serpent impatience that slept always in her belly woke and clattered in its coils as if jibing her: How long, oh my people, how long? But it was not the boy's fault, nor even the father's, if it came to that. It was ignorance, ignorance and superstition and hundreds of years of oppression and the small mean-spirited ways that such oppression bred as if her people were always building smaller and smaller boxes for themselves within the cramped, infinitely small quarters allotted them within the white man's cities and pastures and skies. "I will talk to your father," she promised the boy. "Let us see if we can change his mind on the matter of your schooling."

For a while there was quiet in the kitchen. Miriam grated her carrots and then began to cut a cabbage down into slaw. Sip lost himself to the small in-and-out rhythm of his needle, the little garment that was growing beneath his clever, swift fingers. He'd taught himself to sew but that was nothing, small potatoes. And Mr. Blackburn often brought him off-cuts from the store, shiny bits and bobs of material that the boy allowed himself to examine only when he was alone, running his fingers over a likely piece of rayon or an impossibly shaped but wonderfully gaudy fragment of satin. But where did the inspiration come from, the wind that transformed the boy's clumsy newspaper sketches into the bright coats and frocks of Annabel's summer wardrobe? Perhaps, after all, he was a chosen one, thought Miriam bemused, the enchanted piano player who *would* one day charm the king of Maseru and lead his people out of the House of Bondage and into the Promised Land.

"Bloody!" yelled Ruthie from outside as if in forewarning of her terrible mood. There was the whirr of wheels spinning in dust as she flung her bicycle under the privet and then the front door slammed. When she came into the kitchen she looked more hot than angry, though, her fringe wet with perspiration and her cheeks flushed bright.

"When's he coming home, did he say?"

"Always before dark on a Sunday."

"Except that time last year, but."

"When, meisie?"

"Last year, remember? It was dark already and you said I had to go to bed."

"When he had the puncture, you mean?"

"Well, anyway. Can I have a Coke, Miri, pretty please, just one just one just one?"

"Now think about that question, meisie, think about it. And you won't find the answer in the refrigerator. No, that's where we keep the milk, my girl. And you can have a glass of that anytime you want, according to your father."

Bloody. It was true, Miriam spoke the truth. Her dad had decreed that Coca-Cola was bad for the teeth but milk was good for the bones so she was only allowed one Coke a week and that on a Friday night, but milk, that bland, fizzless liquid beloved of babies and cats, *milk* she could have any time she pleased. Secretly Ruthie was somewhat partial to milk (and besides she was always thirsty these days) but it behooved her to kick up her heels a little, fuss and fret and generally fool around, slamming the fridge door and bumping each chair in turn as she skidded around the kitchen. "Oops! Oh, sorry, Mr. Sipho, didn't see you there."

Sip gazed up at her with his round childish eyes. She frightened him at these times but he was transfixed. She seemed to burn with a terrible energy like an angel or a falling star but he had been taught by his father to turn away from such things, especially the stars that burned and fell with such intensity at the margins of the sky on summer nights.

Nightwatching

"Here, Mr. Sipho, have a glass of milk." Ruthie's mood had changed once again, swerved on its tracks, and before Sip could caution himself she was clinking his glass with her own and diving down deep into her milk, coming up with a thick white moustache and waggling her ears and shrieking with fraudulent laughter. She threw back her head and began to gargle, rocking backwards and forwards in her chair. She seemed to be trying to work herself up to a paroxysm and Sip glanced shyly at Miriam, still standing at the cutting board.

Slowly Miriam whisked her cabbage and carrots into a bowl. "Now I wonder what dressing Mr. Blackburn would like tonight with his coleslaw and sliced salami on rye bread. Could be mayonnaise, could be oil and vinegar. Hard to tell. Last time it was oil and vinegar with caraway seed mixed in, but mayonnaise is good too on a hot night. But the main thing is I mustn't forget to mix the mustard myself from the Colman's packet; that way I can make it strong the way he likes it. Remind me, Ruthie, and also to cut the salami a little bit thicker this time. Hmm, Sip boy, how many Coca-Colas did you say we have in the fridge?"

Sip ran to look, poking his head all the way in and clinking each bottle as he counted. "Four, no, five. Is that enough for the baas, do you think, or must I get more?"

"No, no, five is—" But she hesitated. Mr. Blackburn's

taste for Coca-Cola was legendary and he worked up a thirst like a rabid dog on the dusty road home from Bloemfontein.

Suddenly Ruthie ran to the window. "Listen," she cried. Now they could all hear it, the turning in of a car upon the service road, the slalom of brakes, the wheels changing rhythm as they left the smooth macadam to hitch and grumble on uneven gravel; and they all, each one, stopped in their tracks—Miriam with her brow still curled about the problem of whether or not to set an extra bottle of Coca-Cola in the fridge, Ruthie peering half out of the window, Sip already hovering over the crate of bottles in the pantry, his fingers outstretched—stopped for a moment to listen for the sound of that car slowing as it reached number 67 Unicor Road. Yet the car neither slowed again nor turned into the driveway but continued on its way, a stranger on a stranger's inscrutable journey, and each of the listeners found themselves stranded for a moment in the sudden silence that listening opened in the world.

Well, thought Miriam, soon enough, and Sip ran to lay out the table with salt and pepper shakers and the silver serviette holder and tune the radio that always sat near Mr. Blackburn's place setting to the news station. But Ruthie continued to hang out of the window picturing the moment when the great bottle-green Valiant would turn into the driveway and her dad would stride into the kitchen, one hand held out to ruffle her hair but the other already pulling open the fridge door.

Miriam sat on the low bed in her room in the servant's quarters behind the kitchen. She was reading a letter sent to her by her son Jericho, or rather rereading it because the fact is this letter had been read so many times that its words had already worked little grooves in her brain like the kind that water wears into rock, first by the force of drops and then, as these drops accrue, whole rivulets are worn into the rock and by and by a deluge carries away the very rock itself. For what was this letter but the sum of her boy's hopes and dreams and for how long had he dreamed them in his tiny schoolroom in Thabong Township?

Dear Mama, he wrote, and he went on to wish her good health in the traditional manner for although he was modern in his thinking and radical in his ideas, to his mother he was always her son. And he wrote:

> What's the use of teaching these children to spell and to do their sums? The boys go down the mine shafts and if they're not killed or mutilated in the first five years they'll have another five years of hard labour to look forward to before the mine bosses "pension"

them off, which we both know means cutting them loose without a cent. And the girls are lucky to go into domestic service, lucky, mind you, and after yet another decade of struggle they're still in the same boat that you were in, Mama, when you left school. And there, in some white "Master's" house, they will be forced to bring up his white brats while their own children are sent off to the township because the white Madam can't countenance the fact that her maid is also a woman, a mother, and not merely a servant.

And to these lost children every day I must teach the five-times table and the rules of grammar and the rudiments of the Afrikaans language when it is of history that I wish to speak, and the lessons of history, and the long and weary history of our oppression. It has gotten so bad lately, this hunger of mine to teach our children about their past, that the other teachers make fun of me—I trust it's a gentle humour—and have begun to call me History. So History I've been dubbed and sometimes Jericho the Trumpet and sometimes merely The Call to Arms. Well, perhaps after all the humour is not so gentle but I don't care. I don't care, Mama, because I remember my father's eyes burning fiercely when

Nightwatching

the men came round to our house in those days and talked freely of oppression and proudly of rebellion. And of Karl Marx whose name we can no longer even whisper although his teachings live on, passed between us like a secret handshake between prisoners or grasped hungrily like a piece of bread between starving children. But we are all prisoners, we are all starving.

Mother, I'm sure you know that something has happened or I wouldn't be writing to you with such despair but with hope also and the laughter that shakes a man when he swings from the heights of one to the depths of the other and more than once or twice a day. I have joined the party, the only one that welcomes a black man or woman, and I wait hourly for my orders. Pray God I'll be called to live honourably but you know it's a cause I would die for if I had to. But anything so that this life of mine is of service to my people, anything. If the leaders say to me, "Jericho, our cause is best served by your going back to Thabong School and standing before your school children and starting again from the beginning and saying to them 2 times 5 is 10, 3 times 5 is 15," so be it. And if I must teach them—again— the rules of grammar, that such is a noun and such is a verb, and even if I must teach them the rudiments of the Afrikaans language—although pray God not this last—then *again*, so be it.

But Mother, if I want to be of service to my people it is a long, hard road before me. You know what you must do with this letter and not, under any circumstances, to tell my sister of my calling. I am seeing Jonas this coming weekend and will talk to my brother at that time but about Jonas you need not concern yourself. He's a good and dutiful son but he has told me already that our cause is best served by honest labour. Honest labour, yebo! I intend to give him *Animal Farm*, a book by Mr. George Orwell, and point him towards the character of the sturdy carthorse, Boxer, whose personal motto and answer to every problem was "I will work harder!" Ha! We must work harder—does that not sound like my brother?

Well, Mama, I hope you're in good health. I think of you often and pray that you remain in God's care. My love you have always.

Your son,

Jericho.

When she had finished reading this letter for the last time Miriam arranged it neatly in a little tin can that had once held Golden Syrup and with one long stroke of a kitchen match she set the pages alight. But as they burned she rocked backwards and forwards as if to try to unseat the pain they caused. When the fire had burned itself out she nudged the ashes with the toe of her shoe until nothing at all remained of the letter.

But if a letter could be burned, the anxiety for one's children could not be so easily disposed of. Only last week she had received word from her aunt in the township that Temperance Thandile was refusing to return to school, and, far from being surprised, Miriam was only mildly astonished that such a crisis had not come to pass sooner. For her daughter was of that hasty temperament and impulsive disposition that rendered scholarly pursuits precarious at best. And this was to put it charitably and with all the kindness of a mother's love. "Very bad student" was the consensus of her report cards from the time that she had entered Grade One; "has difficulty with authority" and "takes instruction poorly." But the teachers, when Miriam went to consult with them, were more plainspoken and called the girl rude and defiant and just plain otherwise. And in the staff room, amongst themselves, had she but known it (but Miriam was fully equipped with the imagination to picture the scene and then over and over again in the theatre behind her eyes as she lay alone on her bed after one of these conferences) the teachers were even less tactful and called the child evil.

But she wasn't evil, Miriam thought, not evil but intemperate. Little Temperance Thandile, whom everyone called Temper and at such a young age that she'd had no choice but to grow into her name as a kitten grows into the loose skin at the back of its neck. At five years old she'd knocked a boy out of a tree, younger than her but bigger. Her best friend, and they'd been quarrelling. Well, kids quarrelled. Everyone knew that; they fooled around, got into fights. It wasn't any of those things. It was the way she'd stood over him as he lay on the ground, one foot bent oddly beneath him, and whirled her fists in circles so that nobody could get near him, nobody could approach though the boy was screaming blue murder and it turned out his leg was broken in two places. Still walked with a limp. And later there was a girl whose boyfriend liked her or she liked him. What did it matter? But to end up tussling like that in the dirt of the playground, that, *that* Miriam did not understand. Scratching and slapping, the teachers had reported, and pulling at each other's gymslips and hair and ears. Tcha.

Her brothers had tried to help, they had tried. Jericho had talked to the headmaster to persuade him to lift the suspension and Jonas had gone to the girl's family in a suit and

Nightwatching

tie. "Over a boy," the girl's father had asked, "but why are these two fighting over a boy?" "And over this boy," chimed in the mother. "He is not, after all, a very special boy."

These were questions Jonas could not answer, but Miriam, hurrying home to hold her daughter by the shoulders and stare for herself into her eyes, thought, Well, if not this boy then some other, if not now then next time. It was as plain as the double suns burning in Thandile's eyes and the strange heatedness of her skin when she slept. But at other times her skin was cool to the touch as if no emotions broke the surface of the placid lake she floated on. Shame, thought Miriam, and she began to plan what to do with her daughter because it was clear that, unlike her brothers, she had no feeling for scholarship and her mother was determined that no daughter of hers would feel the hard leather saddle of domestic service upon her back. Still, the child only had a Standard Eight pass. What could she do, what work could she do in the world? Jericho offered to teach his sister at night until she passed her matric and then she could enter the Technikon to learn nursing or even go on to medical school. As he discussed his sister's future over the rickety kitchen table in the shack in Thabong Township, Jericho half closed his eyes as if he must protect himself from the glare of her burnished future and his hands upon his knees opened and shut anxiously.

"No, no," remonstrated Jonas. "Rather we should lower our expectations than set ourselves up for a disappointment. And remember, our sister hates to study. But what about working in a bank or an office reception?"

"And how will this further the cause of our people?" asked Jericho, tapping so impatiently on the table that it rocked across the knees of the three people who sat around it—the two brothers and their mother.

"Tcha, must everything, *every*thing further the cause?" asked Jonas, exasperated.

Jericho just looked at him. Might as well talk to the walls. "Yes," he said. "Yes, everything."

"But she is just a girl," Miriam said. Although she did not say a girl with a bad Standard Eight pass and an even worse temper. "Of course she must still make herself useful," she added hastily as the table rocked so hard across her knees that she had to place both her elbows on its worn surface. But what could she do?

"A shopgirl," Thandile answered when applied to—she wanted to be a shopgirl. She had been dozing in the corner, paying scant attention to the conversation, although it was her future that the brothers were wrangling.

"A shopgirl!" Jericho scoffed. "So you want to become a capitalist pig or better yet an underpaid skivvy for some fat white man's capitalist mode of production? To each according to his meanness, from each according to her greed."

"There's nothing wrong with working in a store," countered Jonas, severely nettled and in the mood for taking things personally. "Even Karl Marx understood the value of an honest day's work. Or if he didn't he should have, and there will be no revolution, *none*, without pride, or are you planning to lead the workers into battle yourself, my brother?"

"Boys," said Miriam holding the table down, "boys . . ." And then, but more softly, "Boys?" A shopgirl, and what was this shop to be and where situated and for how long would her daughter deem this experiment sufficient before she could be persuaded to return to school? Miriam shut her eyes and spoke sharply to the Lord for a moment but then calmed herself and said, "I will talk to Mr. Blackburn, Thandile. I will ask him if he knows of a shopgirl position in this town."

That had been two months ago and Thandile was working in the Concession Store now, apprenticing in Materials and Women's Apparel and it had been good of Mr. Blackburn to take her on, very good. *Very* good, Miriam kept reminding herself nervously though she had realized at once, but too late of course, that by *shopgirl* Thandi meant one of the bold and gaudy assistants in the cheap shoe stores or discount fashion emporiums near the train station or the trinket bazaar lining the street outside the bus depot. These girls tottered about on high heels and flighty self-assurance, their mouths thickened with greasy lipsticks and their laughter brazen with enterprise. No one like that worked for Mr. Blackburn, of course. Just the boys in their shirtsleeves or overalls: Lucas, Wilson, Clanwilliam, Themba. And Jonas, of course, in the backroom with his accounts ledgers and his jacket hung carefully on the wire hanger he kept behind the door.

"I'll keep an eye on her, Mama," he'd promised his mother and this too was very good. A boon, she reminded herself, reminded herself often, and most often when she caught sight of her daughter's face with its habitual expression of discontent and loneliness.

Miriam sighed. For however peevish she was, however stubborn and ungrateful and contrary, Thandile suffered for her waywardness. She was a goodbye-girl, forever waving her careless fingers and setting off without a backward glance, forever leaving her home-broken self behind. But the world was not a stolen bird's egg to be mishandled in some greedy child's hands. "Oh, Temperance," her mother mourned at these times, "be careful, be good, be good." But the wind that blew up off the veld turned her words into a farewell—*goodbye, goodbye.*

Now Temperance Thandile shared rooms with Jonas in

Nightwatching

the Location on the outskirts of town and they travelled together by Putco bus or hitched a ride when they could with a car going on to the mines. On weekends she dressed up and came into town to visit her mama sometimes, but at other times not. Was she happy, was she good? Miriam tried to look into her daughter's eyes to see if the double suns still blazed together but Thandile would not meet her gaze. Would not. Well, and so what? What must a mother do? Miriam prayed and hoped, hoped and schemed, schemed, cursed, repented, dreamed.

Began again.

Ah, but it was late. She must get ready for bed, and tomorrow which would be another day and, like all tomorrows, maybe better.

With some difficulty Miriam climbed up onto her bed to pull the curtains shut because her bedroom window was very small and almost out of reach.

Although her dad had arrived in time for it, supper had not gone well. It was always the way when he came back from one of his trips and Ruthie was trying to ignore the hard little grudge that had settled in her belly like undigested food. Of this last, though, digested or otherwise, she had eaten very little and now she was both hungry and mean-tempered as she crouched under her bush. The house on Bleeker Street, the old Harris house, she thought spitefully, was lit from within by a single lamp and the cracked and dusty lace curtains still framed the back windows.

Ruthie drew her knees up to her chin and began to hum. She narrowed her eyes and the world got briefer but also more vivid as if all that colour and noise had to fit into a postage-sized square of too-small space. Suddenly, from within the house a movement caused her to freeze and hunch inside herself. Someone had come into the living room and walked past the single table lamp, then settled with a scraping of bare floorboards into an easy chair. Gingerly Ruthie put her face to the glass, but the woman, it was a woman and oldish, had her head half turned away from the window. She was leaning her hand against her cheek and reading a book. Ruthie scanned the living room noting how it had changed since the Harrises' occupation. Mrs. Harris had been a ladylike woman, fond of china figurines and flamenco dolls. The living room furniture had been avocado green and in four pieces that fit together like the sections of a child's jigsaw puzzle on a carpet that was the blistering mustard of a late-summer maize field. Ruthie had had much time to contemplate the Harrises' living room with its cunning souvenir clock from the Kimberley diamond mines and its yearly school photographs of the Harris grandchildren, because

Nightwatching

ever since the old man's illness the room had stood empty and she had had all the time in the world to contemplate its vacant acreages.

But now what changes had been wrought and all in the direction of spareness. Gone were the avocado-green jigsaw puzzle of the lounge settee and the mustard rug and the clock, and gone too were all the knickknacks and photographs and ornaments that had fascinated Ruthie in her vigils in the spring when old man Harris was dying up in his bedroom and the living room presented itself to the watching girl as a bright rectangle of light suspended in the night sky. A moving picture though it did not move, a song on the radio though there was no sound. A test pattern to the craven pitch of her longing.

With one swift glance Ruthie saw that the room was bare to the dull parquet floor and the walls were patterned only in unfaded squares of varying size and disposition where once pictures had hung. There was an unfinished, pushed-about look to the room as if a hand had descended and shoved a bookcase against a wall, knuckled the corner rug awry, then thumped a couple of throw pillows together and departed. Willy-nilly Open boxes stood about the room and Ruthie was just craning to see if she could peek at the contents of the nearest of these when the woman in the chair turned uneasily and gazed into the darkness beyond the window.

Well I'll be, Ruthie thought, ducking into the bushes beneath the window, and all the time she huddled there, arms tight around her legs and biting her knee, she kept repeating in her head, Well I'll be, well I'll be, well I'll be, well I'll be. She was truly shocked and nothing seemed to fit the end of the sentence—*darned? damned?*—so she kept repeating the beginning until the words ran into one another and she bit her knee even harder to calm and punish herself both. For she'd neglected the first rule of watching, which was never to stare for longer than a couple of seconds at a time and never directly at anyone. She had trained herself to take in the length of a room with one or two swift sweeps whilst allowing oblique glances at its occupant, and then she would duck back into the shadows and hold the room steady in her mind: the families at supper, the kids playing Ludo on the floor, squabbling or doing homework or wrestling with the dog. If it was summer the windows would be open and then she could hear voices and laughter, radio music, servants washing dishes in the kitchen, a baby crying from a distant room. And now, lately, snatches of excited babble from the television with its tremulous blue light.

Well, she thought, well I'll be! And she bit down until she felt the blood flow that always calmed her with its salty tang and promise of damage done. There were scars on both her knees, scabs on top of old wounds, new sores.

Nightwatching

And scratches on the insides of her elbows, quite deep. Well I'll be!

The woman who'd turned and looked out into the night was Miss Priestly, the librarian. Ruthie was almost certain of it. Same old lumpy sweater, same tight grey hair, same ugly old thing with yellow skin. But not dead; why not dead?

When Miss Priestly had first gone to stay at the hospital in Bloemfontein, Mr. Feinstein gave her "long odds." "She's a tough cookie," he said, "those are the kind that crumble." But her dad wasn't a betting man, just a game of cards with the commercial travellers on a Sunday night, and besides he wouldn't allow wagers on human life. Not in his house. "Take it outside, Jacob," he'd said.

Remembering the conversation that had so excited her at the time—so Miss Priestly was going to die, was she; the dice were loaded—Ruthie felt freshly bewildered. She tongued her bloody knee judiciously and thought hard. But there was no thinking around the fact of her, the librarian, her narrow squint into the dark garden. She was a stone that a thought could not dissolve. So, she tried again, that one has moved into the house on Bleeker Street. The old Harris house.

But it was no use. Ruthie's thoughts parted like water and flowed around the hard and stony fact of her. Well, well.

On Sunday evenings Mr. Blackburn was inclined to attend to his Ledger and this evening, despite the unusual lateness of the hour and Ruthie's turbulence at dinner, was no exception. Oh, Ruthie, mourned Sip from his perch at the kitchen sink where he had been drying dishes, setting each bowl and plate and serving dish down with such care that no surface so much as clinked against another. Indeed, Sip aimed to be the quietest dish dryer that Mister had ever failed to hear, an unfortunate ambition insofar as silence was an often overlooked category of appreciation, Sip was coming to understand. He gazed longingly towards the half-open door of the music room where the piano bared its flashing white grin to the shadows and thought of how Ruthie had taught him to play the "Chopsticks."

Well, she was a teacher of great giftedness, that one! He began on the water glasses, which he had already determined to hand dry with a single clean paper serviette. A feeling of great protectiveness towards Mister bloomed in Sip's chest; he wished he could scrub the kitchen to a sparkling brightness and yet never utter a sound. He wanted to erase the tired lines from around Ruthie's father's eyes, although the manner of doing so escaped him. He longed, so that the very tips of his fingers seemed to buzz, to fill the house with the pure black and white notes that Ruthie, in her infinite kindness, had taught him earlier that day.

Nightwatching

Mister Blackburn, *Mister Black-burn*, he practised, imagining how proud Miriam would be of his memory, his trepidation. Earlier, Ruthie's father had rolled up his shirtsleeves and pulled his chair to the kitchen table. Now his profile, in its stern Sunday-night angularity, was bent over the Ledger. Sip's soft mouth rounded itself into an involuntary O of admiration. Never had he allowed himself to touch the Ledger, but once he'd lowered his head to its cracked green leather and sniffed a quick hard sniff. He would never forget the smell, never, so long as he lived! Smoke, of course, because there was always a cigarette burning to a long cylinder of ash in the saucer as Mister Blackburn worked. And ink, and the dust of the paper on which he wrote down his important money sums. It was the kind of paper that turned your hands grey, and every Sunday after Mister Blackburn had finished his Ledger, he shot his wrists even farther out of their rolled cuffs so that he could scrub his hands pink at the kitchen sink. The grey soap scum twirled down the drain; it carried with it the dust and ash and exhaustion of men. It carried with it the hard glory of earning money.

Sip lowered his eyes with their long lashes because he did not want Mister to look up and catch him watching. "Go home!" Mister might holler. "Why are you still up, you little, you little . . ." Sip's imagination failed him; he did not know what might come after *you little* and his compassion for the older man—for Ruthie's father who had travelled so far tonight and eaten so little supper (although he'd drunk prodigious amounts of Coca-Cola) and even now sat working late into the night—his fellow feeling for this fellow lover of Ruthie rendered him bashful.

Before him on the draining board the three water glasses to which he had pledged himself were in danger of drying haphazardly in the air with all the sins of their water spots and smears fresh upon them. Sip folded his paper serviette along the perforation and sliding his hand inside the first of the glasses began to buff it up to a fine old shine. When he'd finished all three glasses he tilted each one to the light, peering at it with his head canted. There was a piece of dried food that had somehow attached itself to the bottom of the third glass but Sip didn't want to disturb Mister by running the kitchen faucet. Instead he busied himself with a wet thumb and in no time at all he'd detached the food and polished up the water glass once more.

At the kitchen table Mister sighed but it was not the sigh of a man who was about to close his Ledger and shoot his dusty hands from his rolled cuffs. No, it was the sigh of a man in the middle of his important money sums, a man disinclined to stretch or glance up or even lift his head as if at a ghost movement in the shadows. Indeed he did none

Nightwatching

of these things—stretch, glance up, lift his head to catch a stray ghost—when he suddenly cleared his throat and said, "Go home, Sipho. I'll wait up for her."

Mr. Blackburn didn't mean to be stern or dismissive; it was just his way to speak plainly and the kitchen was an echoing room with the tendency of such late-night places to resound more emphatically than in the daylight hours. But with the first word, Sip was a gone-boy, scrambling off his stool by the sink and halfway down the back stairs and already dissolving into the blank-eyed night.

"I'll wait up for her," repeated Mr. Blackburn. Looking up, he saw that he was addressing an empty room. Obscurely ashamed of himself, although he could not exactly say why, Mr. Blackburn rubbed the back of his neck, trying to ease out the kinks. Glancing down he saw that his fingers had left grey smudges of Ledger dust on his shirtfront, but when he hurried to the sink to fetch a glass of soapy water to rinse out the stains, he was astonished to discover three water glasses polished up to such a fierce shine that he quailed at the thought of touching them.

"Now laugh at me if you want, my dear, go ahead and laugh!" Bettina Foley challenged her good friend Annemarie Willems as they swung to and fro on the veranda swing set that wobbled slightly on the music teacher's front stoep. It was the middle of the week and the two friends were taking advantage of a lull in the busy teacher's schedule, for a stubborn summer virus had laid low all but the most robust of her pupils and the weather was too sultry to remain indoors. It was hardly cooler outdoors but Bettina had persuaded Annemarie to try a glass of lemonade with gin and ice rather than their usual pot of strong tea and the two women were more tipsy with the novelty of their weekday get-together than with the unaccustomed alcohol.

Annemarie shifted a little on the seat with its swirling pattern of olive green and white sunflowers. The plastic slipcover was hot and stuck to the back of her legs when she moved but the glass of lemonade was cool and she rolled it ecstatically across her temples. "Heerlik!" Somewhere a bird whirred in a dry bush, the crickets in the veld beyond the highway fiddled their hoarse, off-key bush music, and the seat beneath them creaked fretfully. She felt disinclined to move, to think, to talk, but she knew her friend, she knew old Bettina with her half-coaxing half-nagging ways, so she mustered her reserves.

"Mmm, no, so why must I laugh at you?"

"Well, I've heard from the proverbial little bird that a certain handsome man of our acquaintance is no longer quite as eligible as he once was."

Nightwatching

"Seker!"

"Yes, my dear, quite sekerlik! And that's not all, of course, but are you sure you're interested in my gossip, you sly puss?"

Really, thought Annemarie, her friend had become such a coquette over the years that it was occasionally a trial to have an ordinary conversation with her. She wore tightish skirts for the fashion of a small town in the Free State and stockings even in the summer months, along with her famous, much vaunted Warner's deluxe "two-way" that Bettina swore she had never left the house without. It was perhaps all this constriction that forced her voice up an octave higher than it need be and higher, Annemarie sometimes thought, than any voice had any business reaching for. But as if to make up for the slight unruly thrust of her hips and thighs in their stretched A-line polyester and rayon skirts, she kept a careful rein on her upper body, wearing blouses that buttoned all the way to her chin and barely moving from the waist up. Now Annemarie stretched a trifle irritably and yawned. "Of course, of course, but natuurlik I want to hear all about it."

"Well now, it seems that a certain neighbour of mine, shall we say a certain *widower* who's been in the habit of spending occasional weekends in Bloem, has a new reason to visit our capital city."

Oh, Tina, just tell me the story, Annemarie wanted to say, but she knew better, she'd learned to know better, so—sighing—she arranged her face around the surprise of her half-open mouth. "Oh?"

"Yes, a young lady, or if not *young* exactly . . ."

"But where did you . . .?"

"Oh, I have my sources, don't you worry."

For a while the only sound to be heard was the creak of the swing set as the women swung back and forth in uneasy collusion. But the music teacher was the first to break, she would always be the first to break, her secrecy worth nothing if it wasn't prevailed upon. "Would you like a hint?" she begged.

"Yes, of course," her friend urged; she had held firm and could afford to be gracious. "Do tell, juffie, you always have such up-to-the-minute scandal."

"You know the Oosthuizen boy—Dion? So last week the mother comes in because it's the end of the month and she likes to settle the account and hear how he's doing. Well, did I get an earful, in the course of which I think I hear her mention how perhaps I'm spending too much time trying to teach no-account young girls whose fathers are themselves spending too much time trying to marry no-account older girls and *if* so . . . IF so—

"Well, I thought to myself, enough is enough.

"'Mrs. Oosthuizen,' I said, 'I can assure you that your son is getting all the at*ten*tion and *ex*pertise that he deserves. But if you're dissatisfied with my services then you're very welcome to take your musical requirements elsewhere.'

"'Oh!' she says, and she bites herself in the mouth.

"Now, of course, I'm all the time thinking to myself, Whose father? What marry? Which girl? Mrs. Oosthuizen, she says to me, no, that's quite all right, she wants her Dion to carry on with me but you know how it is, she says, ever since Mr. Oosthuizen passed she's tried to be his mother and his father too. You know how it is.

"'Yes, of course,' I say, and I think I see a way to help her along. 'Ja, being a widow is no easy row to hoe,' I tell her. 'Nor a widower either.' Well, and before you can say Lionel Blackburn, she's off and running. 'Easier for some than for others,' she says. And then she starts to tell me the rumours about how he's been seen in Bloem with this young woman, squiring her here, there and everywhere. To the bioscope and the dances at the Mason Hall and out to dinner at the Golf Course and Country Club.

"'Who is she?' I ask. That's the thing, natuurlik, nobody knows. No one from nowhere, it seems like, although quite good-looking from the sounds of it. And no family to speak of either except a brother in Jo'burg. Convenient, nê?"

"Mmm-hmm." Annemarie's sound of assent was gentle

and undismayed and for a while the two friends swayed companionably together. The ice in the fat jug of lemonade on the table beside them had gone mushy and water droplets beaded the outside. The unaccustomed gin that had made everything bright and fast for a while went flat in Annemarie's blood, lost its fizz and punch, and the world began to slow unnaturally like an LP played at the wrong speed. The impulse to draw her legs up onto the olive and white plastic swing set and go to sleep was difficult to resist.

Somewhere a bird disentangled itself from the afternoon heat to let out a lone and irritable cry that climbed two notes, then picked its way down again. Somewhere a bird and then the sound of thunder too far off to matter and then the bird again. It was afternoon and then it was early evening and then it was dusk.

"Here, bring her here, but? He said that? You sure he said that, Miri?"

"*Uh*-huh."

"When, but?"

"This morning, meisie, I told you already and how many times?"

"No, no, but when, *when* is she coming? And, and but who . . . no, okay, here's what I want to know—" But what

Nightwatching

did she want to know? Too much, everything, all at once. The sky was falling, it felt like, and she was Chicken Little but also the acorn, the fox and the wet red mouth. It was just one of those days. Everything itched. The toast roared in her ears and the sun was a ball that bounced up into her face whenever she gazed outside.

"Your father is bringing home his friend for the weekend. How strange is that?" But even as she spoke, wringing out her dishcloth for emphasis, Miriam thought that it was indeed strange and not just a little. Who was she, this friend? Who were her people? And why must a grown man act the fool in this way, which way could only mean more work for her, for Miriam, who had been instructed to begin airing out the spare bedroom for this Miss Lena, whoever she was. And, as if that weren't all, here was the child wound up like a clock but striking the hour every couple of minutes: *where* would she sleep, *what* would she eat, *how* would she dress? And so on.

"Ag, meisie," snapped Miriam, "do you think she is a doll or what?"

Sip came in and his eyes brightened when he caught the word *doll* but when the situation was explained to him he lost interest and began to lay out his newspaper patterns and a piece of soft blue velvet he'd been hoarding. Ruthie darted here and there unable to settle and Sip kept a wary eye on her. She began to sing a song she'd heard on the radio a couple of days back, first humming the tune and then picking out the words, "Oh! You beautiful doll, you great big beautiful doll! L-e-t me put my arms a-round you . . . Dum dum dum dum dum dum dum dum . . . Oh! You beautiful doll . . . ," over and over but her voice would not, would not settle into the rhythms of the morning and Miriam seized a soft yellow rag in one hand and a long-handled feather duster in the other and hurried out of the turbulent kitchen, her head in an uproar.

Ruthie watched her go and decided not to follow her for although her curiosity about the guest was unassuaged she did not feel like helping Miriam to dust the spare room or make up the bed with sheets from the linen cupboard or roll the vacuum over the rug and then the parquet floor, no not today. What then? Summer cracked and burned outside; it was only ten in the morning but already the shadows were too narrow for comfort. A person had to creep about the edges of things, buildings and fences, trees. That was the kind of summer it had been; endurance gave short shrift. "But it's always this hot, man," she'd heard her dad telling one of the commercial travellers. "This month's always a bloody furnace and nobody remembers again until next year."

Okay, so, okay then. Next year she would try to remember. At night there was no cool place on the pillow and her

Nightwatching

legs ached as if she'd been running barefoot through her dreams and forever. When she'd get up to fetch a drink the water from the faucet was warm and cloudy. Once, on her way back to bed, she passed her father's room and happened to hear him mutter in his sleep. She stopped and waited for him to settle and when he did, the steady in and out of his breathing was peaceful to her and she hunched down in the doorway to his room beyond which she hadn't ventured since three summers ago (she hardly knew why but yet she never did) and she put her head down on her knees and was still and calm. Why, she almost fell asleep like that and was lucky to catch herself before she did, because what would've happened in the morning if her dad had stumbled over her there like a beggar in the doorway? Or Miriam, who was up before either of them. But some nights she couldn't sleep at all and then she'd creep outside and fish her bike out from beneath the privet and make her way along the little side streets and back alleys of the neighbourhood, listening for music or voices from an open window. Or, if she was lucky and it wasn't too late and the lights were still on in the front rooms of a house here or there, she would draw closer and see if she could catch the blue aquarium glow of a television screen. Sometimes there were people still up watching the late news but often there was no one else in the room, just the little box with its underwater light gurgling away.

Miss Priestly, the librarian, had no television set; Ruthie was certain of it now. She'd been keeping an eye on her and only last night had cycled up to the house on Bleeker Street, though she'd had to be very careful, more careful than usual, because the librarian was jumpy with nerves and had kept turning to stare out into the darkness. But she hadn't hung new curtains at the windows; the Harrises' crusty old lace curtains were still up. Perhaps some people needed fear, thought Ruthie. It concentrated the mind and gave the darkness meaning. Or else the new curtains just hadn't arrived yet.

But someone else was staying at the Bleeker house, it looked like. Ruthie hadn't seen her but the night was so hot that the windows were cranked open and, crouched under the rhododendrons, Ruthie had heard a strange voice come into the room and begin talking, quite loud and laughing too. That was how she found out the librarian's name, although she couldn't, at first, believe her ears. Dot! Imagine. Ruthie hadn't known there was such a name in the world, she just hadn't known it. And for such a fatty too, well, why not Splotch, why not Enormous Circle, why not Hemisphere? She'd had to stuff her hand into her mouth and shut her eyes tight and wait for the giggles to ease their way out of her shaking body, but it had taken time.

There was something else too and this something had

Nightwatching

to do with the night of the Benders' party, which she tried not to think about because at the end of it, at the end of the swimming pool and the dancing couples and the music and the cocktails and the fairy lights, there was the man with his hairy bum leapfrogging the woman and the panting breaths of the man and the squeals of the woman and a sudden chemical stink like swimming pool chlorine. Would the librarian—Dot!—would she squeal like that, like *that*, and did the librarian—oh no, surely not!—did this mean that the librarian also had a hairy bum?

She'd lain for a while in the dark trying to make sense of this leap—why the terrible creature that she'd encountered in the dark of the Benders' garden so often sprang into her mind and superimposed itself onto the faces and bodies of the adults she knew, so that she was always confused and disheartened, reciting "Ozymandias" to herself or giggling helplessly until her stomach hurt and her heart rattled and her breath wouldn't come. Bloody. Anyway, the other voice, a sort of fat old voice too   Ruthie imagined another large polka Dot—this other voice had come into the room and called the librarian up to bed, and so that was that and Ruthie had gotten home early enough but she hadn't been able to sleep and now she was buggered.

Sip was still busy with his patterns. He'd leaned Annabel against the silver serviette holder and was cutting a piece of maroon satin into the outline of a pair of trousers with wide flares. As he worked he hummed and bit his thread cleanly and quickly as he did everything in his quick, clean way. From the interior of the house Ruthie could hear Miriam sneezing again and again as she always did when she dusted and then an exclamation—"yoh weh!"—and then more sneezes. My dad is bringing home a, a guest, she thought. And then: We are preparing our house for a guest. Guest, a *Guest*! This was the word she hadn't imagined until this moment, until just this very moment, and then it was—she realized this now—the right word, the only word that would do. It was what she had been, all her life, waiting for.

Sip was sitting under the thorn tree by the abandoned water reservoir. He had come in search of his Ruthie, propelled by a queasy mixture of love and restlessness. Love ticked within him as steadfastly as the hour hand around which the restless minute hand of a kitchen clock revolved in tight, overlapping circles. The world shimmered and pulsed with heat, and still Sip sat trying to remember what had confounded him. For a while it escaped him and for a while it pursued him but there was no time at all in which the elusiveness of his thoughts kept pace with their desire. It had something to do with fathers, but.

Nightwatching

There was Mister, alone in the night kitchen, doing his Ledger. His profile was as curt and absorbed as the profile on a coin but when Sip pictured Mister he was beset by the same melting tenderness of heart that had caused him to pocket the square of paper serviette with a mind to tackling the water glasses later that evening. And there was his own father, of course. But in all the world, thought Sip, surely there could not be two fathers less alike. Yet both—here he hunched into himself and closed his eyes so as to think his thoughts—yet both seemed to require his care just as Annabel did, although Annabel smiled her thanks constantly and with supreme tact.

The thorn tree was a scraggly old thing and the sun was hurtling about in the sky today so Sip had to hunch to fit himself into a child's scribble of shade. No, *the earth*, he thought suddenly, remembering how Ruthie had laughed at him.

"It's the earth that circles the sun, stupid. Well, you are an Egotist, aren't you, Sipho my boy! Thinking that the sun and all the planets revolve around you, tcha."

Ruthie had called him one, so Sip was proud to be an Egotist, but he didn't want to make the same mistake twice. "The *earth* around the *sun*, the *earth* around the *sun*," he whispered into his cupped hands. When he'd finished he thought he would empty his bladder and looked for a tree or clump of bushes large enough to shield him. There was no one to see but still he didn't like to *make a spectacle of himself* as he had once heard Miriam bully a couple of men in the park. His favourite thing was to watch the dull copper of the earth turn bright red under his stream.

It was strange because it only took a couple of seconds but when Sip came out of the bushes the sun had swung behind a cloud and the sudden darkness had silenced the insects, perhaps, because the buzz and crackle of the veld, so insistent that you could only hear it when it was gone, had ceased entirely. Sip trotted back to his thorn tree. He sat and drew his knees up to his chin the way he'd seen Ruthie do. First it worked and then it didn't quite. His heart was banging about in his chest; it was a bird that had blundered into a room and couldn't get out. The silence, the sudden darkness—was this what had frightened him so? Sip pulled the top of his T-shirt away from his neck and peered inside. The sight of his thin little chest calmed him suddenly. With all his heart he'd wanted to come to the water reservoir and find his Ruthie sitting beneath her bush. Once it had happened and so might again.

But the truth was that he didn't like the water reservoir. Plain didn't. And this was because of the great rusting bulk of it rearing into the air. Sometimes from about a mile away, as he walked across the veld, Sip could see the whole of the reservoir outlined against the horizon on its

Nightwatching

splayed struts. But by the time he drew near, by the time he crouched beside it as he was doing now, he had to crank his head so far back to glimpse the top of the vast cylindrical drum that he was in danger of toppling over, and often did.

Now, righting himself, Sip averted his thoughts from the reservoir towering above him. And the dark oily water inside, and even worse. The worse was what sometimes fell in and couldn't get out again, which Sip didn't like to think about. So didn't.

Instead he thought about Annabel and the new trousseau that he was sewing for her. He'd been saving the piece of blue velvet for a "going-away," a piece of cloth that he rubbed against his imagination at moments like these. Annabel in his heart smiled her fond smile, but the sun remained dark and the veld so silent that he could hear the electricity hissing in the pylons and the smell in the air was not at all bridal. No, it was the bloated green stink of what something became after a week in the tank.

Sip closed his eyes and concentrated on love. Then he scrambled from beneath his thorn tree and chased his careening shadow all the way home.

"But, but what does she do?"

"Do?" Her dad looked over the top of his newspaper

as if he were really saying *Who?* and as if this were just an ordinary day, a day upon which he would soon wipe his mouth on his serviette and say, "Excuse me, ladies, I'll see you after work." But it wasn't that sort of day at all and no one was going to work today, or at least her dad wasn't. They were all hanging around the kitchen waiting for her dad to get ready to fetch the Guest from the bus station. It was early yet but Ruthie was feeling anxious and getting more so with every minute that revolved around the tight red face of the little kitchen clock.

Everything was slightly at odds today, capricious and awry. Ruthie seemed to have grown two inches in the night and now her denims were the only shorts she could wear that decently covered her legs. Even so she was uneasily aware of her poky knees, so like a boy's, scratched up and bony. And her hair that she had tried to brush one hundred times every night of the summer—or anyway those nights that she remembered or wasn't too tired to manage, and certainly last night—her hair remained what it had always been: tow-coloured, fly-away, rebellious. But mostly what Ruthie was anxious about was the state of her footwear. Since she no longer possessed sandals that fit, she'd gotten up early and whitened her tennis shoes until they creaked, but she remained dubious about the propriety of wearing mere tennis shoes in the presence of the Guest.

"Do?" her dad said. "She works in a bank. Loans and Savings."

Ruthie bit at the ragged cuticle of her thumb and worried her toast into crumbs. But how had he met her, she wondered, and what had happened at this first meeting to bring about this extraordinary circumstance, this strange Saturday morning—the first she'd ever known—when her dad wasn't dressed for work, his sports jacket neatly hung on the back of the chair and his shirtsleeves rolled once to keep them out of the way of his porridge? Instead he sat there in his weekend trousers and blue golf shirt that was too bright in the sleepy morning kitchen. The shirt made everything in the kitchen seem dull and a little mournful: the scuffed linoleum, the breakfast dishes pushed this way and that on the sticky oilcloth with its puddles of milk and tea, the transistor radio on the windowsill with its tinny voice announcing, "Another scorcher, listeners, looks like another record-breaking high!" And even Miriam standing with her hands in the sink seemed slow and dreamy and not at all herself.

A fly fretted the kitchen curtains and Miriam took up the swatter and went after it. Her dad jiggled the knob of the radio until he found a news station but even then he didn't leave off reading his paper. Last night when she hadn't been able to sleep Ruthie had thought hard about the Guest, her mind skittering about in the dark from one thing to another, the way it had done all day but faster. Perhaps she'd resemble the heroines of the photo romances that were displayed in racks at the front of the Greek Caffy and which Ruthie always paged through when she bought gum or sweets, although she had to be quick because old Papadopoulos hated the kids to touch them and had a voice that thundered and a terrible accusing finger. The women in these photo romances were beautiful but troubled because they were often pursued by no-good suitors who gathered them up in inky close-ups that came off on her fingers. Ruthie couldn't imagine her father as one of these suitors though, she just couldn't. Well, and what about that awful woman on the radio drama that she and Miriam sometimes listened to, *For Infamy and Bliss*? Perhaps the Guest spoke in a high, lisping voice and giggled all the time and *ate men for breakfast*, as one of the heroine's lovers had accused her of doing. *Chewed them up and spat them out.* Ruthie tossed and turned.

But in the morning she'd become preoccupied with her terrible shorts and her poky knees and whether her tennis shoes were all right and damping her fringe down. The phone rang in the hall and her father went off to answer it and she could hear him laughing and joking with someone. It sounded like Mr. Feinstein. "No, man," he was saying,

Nightwatching

"leave it to Jonas, why don't you. The boy's got a head on his shoulders." And then a pause and more laughter. "Okay, I'll see you Monday morning. Noon at the latest."

Miriam was still following a fly dreamily around the kitchen with her fly swatter held at the ready. Well! Sometimes she got into these moods but not often. More often she was good old Miriam tumbling cups one into the other, sloshing the water about in the sink and polishing up the dining room furniture. Even her dad looked surprised at Miriam's indolence when he walked back into the kitchen.

"Hmm, lots to do around here still, hey. And what time did I say I would fetch Miss Lena from the bus station?"

"Ten-thirty," said Ruthie, surprised, because surely he hadn't forgotten? No, but it was just his way of hastening the morning along, shaking Miriam from her lethargy and Ruthie too, who was cupping her chin in her hands and staring at the ceiling again, which she always did when she thought something through or tried to, from beginning to end—Miss Lena, Miss Lena, Miss Lena . . . From the open window a musical scale climbed up and down brokenly and it seemed to the listeners that it was the voice of the heat itself, huffing and panting with effort. "Again," called the music teacher, "again."

Outside the morning shimmered and shook. You couldn't look at it straight on or it would blur and disappear at the edges, or else you would. One of the two, but the invisibility this morning was bad. Out on the highway the cars flubbed past and the sound they made blended into the heat and became something you could cut yourself on if you ventured outside without a hat or sunglasses or at least a hand visored up to your brow. An engine detached itself and rattled down the gravel service road, driving fast. It hardly slowed at all when it reached the driveway but still it turned in to number 67 and Ruthie, running up to the window, was the first to see the bright red car pull up to the house. It arrived in a cloud of dust but somehow the dust—how was this possible? . . . she thought later but couldn't figure it out—the dust couldn't diminish the brightness of the little red car or the gay jangle of music from the car radio or the two people who, even as she watched, were climbing out.

A man first, tall and dark, and he hurried to the passenger door to help the lady. The lady was wearing big sunglasses and a jaunty motoring kerchief and she had one hand on the hooter, honking to say they'd arrived, and the other lifted up so the man could pull her out of the car. Even from the kitchen Ruthie could sense the laughter that tossed her about as if the world were a joke that she was enjoying and with all her heart. She threw back her head again and laughed then hooted two more short blasts.

"Ho-ly," exclaimed her dad and hurried outside.

Nightwatching

"No, but really, Lionel, Syl had the weekend off and he said let's surprise them by driving down early. So what do you think of our little surprise? I told him you'd be shocked, nê?" The woman was quite tall, almost as tall as her dad, and the hair beneath the kerchief that she pulled off as she spoke was dark and curly. "Oho, what have we here?" she said, looking at Ruthie and still trying to fix her hair but laughing helplessly because of the wind knots.

"Ruthie, say 'how do you' do to Miss du Toit," said her dad, and she saw how nervous he was because he never told her what to say, never.

"No, no, that's all right, just give your Auntie Lena a kiss, there's a girl." Her cheeks were very smooth and she smelled fragrant, sweet and powdery and smoky all at once, like perfume and cigarettes and Sen-Sen and baby powder and sun and dust.

By now the woman called Lena had giggled her merry way into the house. "Syl," she called through the open kitchen window, "man, bring the luggage in, okay?" She wore a yellow pantsuit, bright like the yolks of eggs or the centres of daisies, and the legs of her trousers had subtle flares that flapped as she walked. But the most beautiful thing of all was a gold bracelet that clattered with charms as she waved her hand about, which she did all the time, back and forth and round about, as if she herself liked nothing better than

{195}

to watch the hearts and shamrocks, proteas, thimbles, and music notes bobble on her wrist.

Miriam began to clear off the breakfast dishes but she wasn't quick enough and Ruthie worried about the kitchen's disarray, the sink still full of grey soapy water and the mess of wet tea leaves in the pot. She ran from one thing to another, distractedly trying to set things to rights, sweeping toast crumbs into her hand and rushing into the scullery to push the ironing board out of sight, then darting back into the kitchen to check on the flypapers. Had they been changed lately? Oh!

"Humba," Miriam scolded. "Get out!"

"No, but . . ." But Miriam was firm and uncommonly sombre and she pushed the girl into the hall, from where Ruthie could hear the rise and fall of the woman's voice—she was still laughing—and her father's deeper laughter running beneath. She stood very still, first on one leg and then the other. But what were they laughing about? A great loneliness seized Ruthie suddenly and she was as a tiny, burnt-out star in the vast cold immensity of space, lost even to herself.

"Welcome to Welkom, goats and monkeys!"

Syl had come up behind her and was standing in the front door with luggage under his arms. The morning light blazed across the threshold and threw his face into shadow but Ruthie could hear the laughter in his voice.

Nightwatching

"Goats and monkeys!" he shouted again and with one stride was inside the hall and the woman with the charm bracelet came running to meet him from the lounge, dragging her dad by the hand.

"Let's make a proper family weekend of it, Lionel, skat. Syl can stick around till Sunday afternoon, then drive me home again. He doesn't care where he sleeps, do you, boet?"

"I do not," agreed the man called Syl. "Wherever I hang my hat is home." He tipped off his peaked cap as he spoke and hung it backwards on Ruthie's head. He had brown curly hair like his sister and smooth tanned skin and a fine line of hairs beneath his nose and above his soft full lips. His cap felt warm still, unpleasantly so, and Ruthie yanked it off but then felt bad when he caught her holding it gingerly with the tips of her fingers. He winked at her.

"Ruthie, go and tell Miriam to make up the spare cot in the card room," her dad told her. "It's very comfortable," he explained to Syl as she skidded through to the kitchen, "and in the summer—"

"Miriam," she hissed, "she's gone and brought her brother. You've never seen such a moustache!" A sense of enjoyable calamity possessed her. "And you must make up the cot in the card room, he says, but what'll we feed them all?"

"Tcha, what nonsense are you talking now, meisie? Is there not enough food in the house?"

"No, but he looks very hungry, Miri, you've never seen such a face. Like a, like a dog panting for its supper." The devil had gotten into her and suddenly she was in the mood to plague Miriam. "Sies, just look at the mess in this kitchen, man, what are they going to think, those two? I bet you they have a clean kitchen in Bloemfontein and so much food they don't know what to eat first. And, and Coca-Cola just whenever they want it." As she scolded, Ruthie slammed around the kitchen opening cutlery drawers and knocking them shut again, poking her head into cupboards and colliding with the edge of the table and her own hasty cantankerousness. Miriam ignored her, but she was neither angry nor hurt for she'd caught the tug of loneliness that had set poor Ruthie adrift, set her tumbling and whirling through space and the barrenness at the margins of other people's companionship.

A burst of laughter from the lounge seemed to galvanize her. She rushed into the music room and tore open the lid of the piano. Eagerly she began to play "Chopsticks," thumping out the counterpoint with crashing chords and throwing herself against the melodic line, again and again, until it yielded before her will and she was done. A silence had fallen when Ruthie began playing and when she was done the silence went on a little longer and then there was a sort of snorting sound as of someone trying not to laugh

Nightwatching

but not trying sufficiently. But then clapping also, and the man's voice shouting "Brava! Brava!"

Ruthie, that mad girl, began to play "Chopsticks" again.

". . . see the store?" Mr. Blackburn was saying, "and then lunch in town and perhaps the Botanical Gardens in the afternoon."

But by the time Ruthie had begun "Chopsticks" for the fourth and loudest time, the red sports car was reversing down the driveway once more and a great and echoing silence had descended on the kitchen.

The afternoon was an open mouth that yawned. Ruthie hung around the house reading old adventure annuals and picking at the scab on her knee. Miriam let her have a bottle of Coca-Cola but it only made her more thirsty afterwards and she had never known time to pass so slowly. Whenever she looked at her wristwatch thinking surely an hour had passed, probably two, only five minutes had crept by on shuffling, dragging feet. Sometimes not even. The phone didn't ring and no one came to the door and Miriam took the radio out to the yard with her to where she sat with the maids who visited with their babies on Saturday afternoons. From the kitchen came the sound of the women talking Zulu and their laughing babies and the radio tuned to an African music station but the rest of the house was silent except for a fly caught between the windowpane and its own fretfulness, and the roof ticking in the afternoon sun.

Soon they'll be back, Ruthie thought to herself. She yearned towards the highway anticipating, in the sound of each approaching vehicle, the one that would turn off the macadam and along the gravel service road and then bump and jolt onto the driveway. But the cars on the highway drummed past every ten minutes or so and though her apprehension strained out and towards them so that she felt as if she were a giant eardrum listening for the first crunch of loose gravel, the first hitch of wheels and chafe of brakes, yet the silence stretched on and on. Ruthie turned a page but she'd lost the thread of her story, and though she read the same sentence over and over again it made no sense to her. Suddenly she could bear it no longer, the silence, the afternoon swinging loosely about its axis, the sense of her own grievousness. She slammed her book shut and ran outside.

A bird slid up two notes and down again, over and over, with a sweet monotony. Ruthie grabbed her bike and made for the park—where else was there to go? The heat blazed up out of the dust road and roared across the street to the roofs of the houses on either side so that she had to slit her eyes and pedal for all she was worth. But when she got there the park was flashing with painful light and everything was hot to the touch: the metal chain links of the kids' swings and the blistering paint-cracked frame of the monkey bars and the long, aching curve of the slide.

Only Dion and Sip were in the park, playing marbles in the dirt by the merry-go-round. Ruthie went to join them, balancing herself on the merry-go-round although she had to be careful not to touch the blazing metal with her skin. Even through her shorts it hurt but she was no baby, no siree. Dion looked at her without enthusiasm, but Sip was happy to see her and gave her a shy half smile. Sip was setting up a shot. It was a tricky one because what was at stake was Dion's prize goon, a king-size marble with topaz and amber swirls through milky glass.

"What would you rather?" he asked Sip. "Would you rather kiss a boy or be a girl?"

"I would rather be a girl," said Sip. He took careful aim, bending so that the side of his head was flat against the ground. But when he shot his marble it curved off at the last moment and the goon was safe.

"Ag, sies, that's not the right answer," Dion was trying to explain. "No, man, who wants to be a girl?"

"Ha, so, Dion, you want to go around kissing boys now? I thought so!" Ruthie was exultant. She leaned her arms on her thighs and rocked with laughter. Too late, Dion realized the trap he'd fallen into but there was nothing he could do because that terrible Ruthie was pressing her hand against her mouth and pretending to smooch herself, making wet kissing sounds and screaming with laughter.

"That's okay," he said sulkily, "because no one's gonna kiss you. Never. And you'll die of ugliness and, and *stink*iness."

But he was almost crying with mortification and it was too hot to fight him, so Ruthie thought, okay, she'd just twist his arm behind his back or give him a Chinese bracelet or a pinkie burn, but later. Got you back.

"But still," said Sip, "I would rather be a girl. I would rather be a girl and wear beautiful clothes and high-heeled shoes. And have a lilac wedding dress like Miss Elizabeth Taylor and round sunglasses like Miss Jacqueline Bouvier Kennedy." As he spoke he lined up his marbles and shot them off one by one with great accuracy or a sudden access of luck because in no time at all he'd picked off all of Dion's marbles including his prized goon.

"But are you mad? Are you sick? What kind of a person wants to wear girl's clothes?" Dion was flush with indignation, and to make matters worse, all he possessed now in the way of marbles was a handful of charmless ball-bearings of various sizes that rolled about listlessly in the dust.

"I would," said Sip simply. "I would if I was a girl."

"Oho, my little man, if you're so interested in girl's clothes then it's a pity you missed my friend, Miss Lena du

Toit. Boy, is she ever something. Well, when I saw her I said to myself, now there are some clothes for you, those are the most fascinating clothes that have ever been worn in this town. Yes, if there was a prize given for beauty then it would have to go to Lena du Toit and her fascinating clothes. Oh and, hmm, here's how she walks—"

Scrambling up, Ruthie swayed from side to side on the path before them, thrusting out her hips and scowling with concentration. "And *this* is how we danced last night at the discotheque and then we each had a bourbon cocktail, only I had two because I was *so* thirsty. Well, I can certainly recommend a bourbon cocktail if you ever find yourself thirsty after dancing all night at the discotheque, I can certainly do that."

The two boys looked at her with wide eyes, then each made a decision at exactly the same moment. "Rubbish!" yelled Dion, but Sip pulled at her arm with shy eagerness and asked, "What did Miss Lena wear to the disco?"

"Sequins," said Ruthie quickly. "Well, obviously a tube top with sequins all over is what you wear to a discotheque, stupid."

"So what did *you* wear, *stupid*?" asked Dion.

"Also a tube top, sequinned. And stovepipe jeans?" Sip spoke dreamily as if his words conjured the billowing smoke and sequins and flashing lights of their shared fantasy from out of the scrappy kids' park with its rusty merry-go-round and dusty trees.

"Ag, what's the difference, you weren't there." Suddenly she was bored with her game. "Who wants to go play tok-tokkie?"

"Okay," said Dion, and with a businesslike shake of his head he motioned Sip to return his marbles.

Sip, who'd known they were not his to keep, had them at the ready. It was always this way; no matter how his luck held or how many marbles he'd won he knew that, at the end of the game, he must return them to Dion and all would be as it had ever been.

The concrete backyard behind the Blackburns' kitchen was noisy with the sound of laughing women and gurgling babies and even the cajoling notes of a jazz trumpet issuing from the radio with only a small amount of static. Every Saturday afternoon the women gathered back there and the sound of their merriment was one of the reasons that Bettina Foley took herself off to the weekly bioscope with Annemarie Willems for, as she told her friend, it was like a shebeen back there and the palaver made her head want to split in two. No, really, when she thought of that nice Mr. Blackburn, they must be stealing him blind. Tea—was it?—that his uppity kitchen girl was offering around, just like the madam she must think she was. Truly, it was better that she just packed up and left every Saturday afternoon; you'd have to be deaf, dumb and blind not to resent it and, yes, she wouldn't tell a lie, resent it she did.

"Ag, soentjie, have a little chocolate," her friend consoled her, offering the box of Black Magic soft centres. But what could you do? They were all around you these days and they had taken over the world.

If the women in the Blackburns' backyard had overheard this peevish conversation they would have laughed heartily as they did at most things, throwing their heads back and letting the tears roll unchecked down their cheeks. *Hau! Shew weh! Yoh yoh yoh!* As it was they found much to laugh at and hilarity ran high on this as on most Saturday afternoons when Miriam brewed tea or passed around bottles of Coca-Cola or ginger ale. Sometimes bought biscuits, sometimes made. One thing about Mr. Blackburn was that he didn't mind how generous Miriam was with the contents of his cupboards; he hardly noticed how swiftly the crates of Coca-Cola disappeared or how often packets of tea and sugar were replaced.

"And what do you hear from Jericho?" asked Annie, dandling her new baby proudly. She'd once had a passion for Miriam's oldest son and she still liked to fasten a benevolent eye on his comings and goings, but from a distance as of one who shakes one's head gently from side to side. Ho, that boy!

"He is very well, thank you," said Miriam, "but not married naturally because if he was you'd have heard me crying the good news from the top of this roof."

Under cover of the burst of approbation that followed her words, Miriam gazed about at the smooth round heads bobbing on their mothers' arms or drooping sleepily from blankets tied across those broad backs and felt her heart slide hungrily around the emptiness of what she longed for. "*Uh*-huh."

"And tell me, Mama," asked Sophie, "how is Thandile enjoying her job? I am hearing great things about this new shopgirl position. Even that she is so good at inviting customers into the store that the mine boys are queuing up around the block on a Saturday afternoon."

The women gasped. This was too much—a cruel half-truth barbed as a fish hook thrown out to catch at the tender flesh of Temperance's mother. And wielded by a woman whom everyone knew to be vengeful for no reason other than her own misfortune in the way of a barren womb and a fecund imagination.

But Miriam, as was her way, as was always her way, remained calm and even-tempered. "My daughter, Temperance Thandile is well, thank you for asking. She is a very good store clerk and I am proud of her. We are all proud of our children, which is a mother's blessing."

And now the women gasped again but this time in awe at the manner in which Miriam had plucked the barb from her own skin while lightly grazing that of the other woman. Quickly, gentle Annie applied a general balm, changing the subject by asking after Jonas, of whom all the ladies approved, and there was much clicking of tongues and exclamations of fondness. A baby wailed and Miriam offered to take him from his mother, after which he soon quieted for she had a magic touch; her strong hands seemed made for cupping and the crook of her arm was the safe, sure harbour against infant storms.

Miriam dropped her head and breathed in the sleeping baby while around her the women laughed and argued and drank tea and sipped Coca-Cola from the bottle. It had been a hot, dusty Saturday afternoon like so many others that summer, but the Blackburns' backyard was inclined to coolness, being paved with concrete and sectioned off with high walls that threw harsh lines of shadow across. Every Saturday afternoon of that summer the women had come with their babies and sat in the shade of the kitchen wall, braiding each other's hair and gossiping, scolding one another mostly to tease and sometimes to wound, but this last not often. When the cold weather came they would not be so punctual, although every now and then a sunny Saturday would bring the women out to the backyard again in their jerseys and overcoats. As the months passed, more and more babies would be missing from the roll call. Too old to stay with their mothers, the madams would say, so they'd have to be sent back to the homelands, to a grandmother or an aunt.

Looking about her, Miriam missed them already: the tight, curly pelt of their heads, their round, hot Milo-coloured eyes.

"You go."

"No, you."

"Fat chance, boys. I already said. So one of you better decide." Ruthie pushed her fringe away from her damp forehead and squinted at the two boys. Sies, man, eight-year-olds! They were both such babies. "Or we can just go back home. *I* don't care, I've done this lots of times already. You think I care fuck all for being caught? Because no way that's gonna happen. So make up your bloody minds or let's just get the hell out of here, you little wet-pants crybabies." Ruthie paused admiringly. She liked to curse some when she could, although seldom had she produced such an unbroken stream of invective.

The three children had trudged through town squeezed

between the blaring sun and the heat that still roared up at them from the pavements. They had pooled their resources at the Greek Caffy and bought a cream soda with three straws but it had only lasted two pulls each and left them feeling sweet and sticky and subtly discontented and it had begun a quarrel that endured all the way up Bleeker Street to where they now crouched in the vacant lot in front of the old Harris house arguing about who would be the first to knock on the librarian's door then run away.

"You."

"No, you."

Tok-tokkie was an ancient sport, as old as the town itself, and the rules were simple. Knock and flee, knock and flee; repeat until the householder gave futile chase or was driven mad or disappeared in a puff of smoke. Whichever came first. Sometimes the houses were chosen at random but more often it was a game of grudges played out by the neighbourhood children on long hot afternoons that seemed to whip out of one's hands like the tail end of a hosepipe.

"All right," said Sip as if he were finally making up his mind. But of course he'd known who would be tok-tokkie. All of them knew and right from the beginning too. He closed his eyes for a moment and remained quite still, then flung himself across Bleeker Street. There was a garden gate but it was unlatched and then a polished stoep and a front door with three diamond panels cut out of it, and upon this front door—turquoise to match the guttering going up one side of the house and down the other—upon this front door Sip threw himself for all he was worth. Even in the vacant lot across the street Ruthie and Dion could hear the bright hard rap of his knuckles on the door frame and they waited with their hearts jumping about in their chests. But nothing happened and nothing happened and nothing happened. And even when Sip came pumping across the road and climbed into the ditch with them and all three continued to stare at the house, nothing still happened for so long and for so hard that it was as if nothing were a thing that *could* happen, as if the hot blue day and the veld that itched their legs and the rasp of the everlasting crickets were just the frame for the nothing that would go on and on.

"No one there," said Dion finally.

"Yes, there was," said Sip too quickly.

"No one there," agreed Ruthie. "Can't have been."

"Yes, there was, there *was*." Sip felt close to tears.

"Can't have been, stands to reason." Ruthie swiped at her fringe again and surveyed the boy. Well, what was bothering him now? He gulped and gulped and rubbed his knuckles against his eyes. Suddenly she came to a decision. "All right, Sip my little man, here's the deal. You go do tok-tokkie one more time and if—*if* you can get her to come to the door then you win, okay?"

He didn't quite say *Win what?* but he looked it, so Ruthie grabbed a handful of marbles and stuffed them in her pocket. "Here, you can have some of Dion's marbles."

"Hey," whined Dion, but like Sip he was powerless before the force of her soldered will.

Pocketing his hands Sip hunched across the street again. He darted through the gate and up the path and when he got to the turquoise front door he put his ear to its surface and listened gravely. No, nothing. So he shrugged and lifted his fist to do tok-tokkie, half turning so that they could see his wide grin because he had nothing to lose and everything (marbles) to gain and this, this turning, this grinning, the half-wave that he'd half lifted his hand to begin on, was the reason he failed to see the door swing silently open, very slowly at first, just a chink of shadow at the edge of the door frame, before a hand groped out and grabbed him, gotcha!

Damn, thought Ruthie, bloody bloody bloody!

Dion was tugging at her to run; he wanted to get the hell away. Although why? thought Ruthie, it wasn't as if the hand behind the door could get them too; they were quite safe hidden in the ditch and she wanted to see what would happen next. She'd have died if she couldn't have, just died.

Later, when she'd had time to think it all through,

Ruthie decided that the hand had been hiding on the other side of the turquoise door, drawn slyly down by that first tok-tokkie. And all that time, waited. Imagine that! It boggled the mind, not a word of a lie. And who, who . . . ?

The hand that was grasping poor Sip at the back of his neck began to shake him up and down so that his head bobbled about like a silly toy dog on a dashboard. And as it shook him backwards and forwards and round and about, a voice from behind the door, high-pitched and breathless, started to yell: "Picannin, picannin, picannin! What are you doing here, you bloody bloody picannin, with your picannin bloody nonsense and your bloody picannin cheek?"

"Whoa!" said Dion beside her, impressed but shitting himself too, and he clambered out of the ditch and ran for it.

Sip had begun to wail but there was so little air left in him that he rattled and gasped and made a little *eew eew* like a punctured balloon. Suddenly the front door swung wide and the—no, but not the librarian—the other one stood there, grim and bun-haired and *thin*. Ruthie had never seen her before and for a moment she was so taken aback by this thinness that she forgot everything else, the gasp of the mad boy deflating on the doorstep, the itch of the veld grass against her knees, and the shrill cry of "Picannin, picannin, picannin!" She'd heard this voice once before when it had called the librarian Dot—Dot!—

Nightwatching

and it had been a fat and hummy voice that plumped up the gentle breezes of the summer's night and wafted them past the window where she lay listening. So, but, who was this, this, thin-as-a-rake, boney-as-a-witch, fierce-as-two-crossed-sticks somebody who was still shaking poor Sip, although it seemed she was running out of breath at last? Beneath her anger she seemed strangely familiar but Ruthie had no pause to consider resemblance.

"Run!" Ruthie suddenly flung herself out of the ditch. "Yah, picannin yourself," she shrieked at the woman. "Yah, you old blue-arsed witch!"

The woman released Sip and fell back against the door frame. Her mouth opened in a long O of shock but no sound came out, although half her hair tumbled in rough grey swags from her bun.

"Run!" yelled Ruthie again, and this time she jumped up and down to attract Sip's attention, or try to, because the boy was crouched motionless on the doorstep like a bird that had smashed full tilt into a windowpane. Well, what must she do? thought Ruthie. But she couldn't just leave him there.

"Sipho! Sipho!" she shouted, and she picked up a stone and threw it at him and then another.

The woman was still leaning against the door frame, panting, with one hand clutching her chest but for who knew how long.

"Sipho!" shouted Ruthie again but it was no use, the boy was stunned unto kingdom come and there was nothing for it but she must run across the road and pull him to safety, damn his black heart. She was already halfway across by this time and then she was crashing through the gate and down the garden path in a chaos of dust and noise, one arm outstretched so as to snatch him away.

Sip saw her coming and at last roused himself to move but sluggishly and without volition. The woman saw her coming too and drew herself up to her full height, making a grab at Sip with one hand and with the other trying to catch at the hairpins that were jumping from her head, but the hair continued to unscrew itself in all directions until in a frenzy of despair she simply put both hands to the welter of pins and net and falling hair and called out in a terrible lost voice: "Dot, ag, Dot, my love, come save me!"

Ruthie barely heard the clatter from within or the sound of the librarian's voice added to the other woman's because she'd grabbed Sip and was pulling him across the road by now, and he seemed to have finally gotten the measure of her panic and was pumping his thin arms up and down, jerking his idiot boy's heels across the short veld grass of the vacant lot to where the fence gave way and they could scramble through. Ruthie grabbed the handlebars of her bike and pedalled for all she was worth and Sip ran alongside

Nightwatching

of her until he couldn't keep up anymore and she had to go back for him, but by that time Bleeker Street was long gone.

"Nice try," said Ruthie, "but why didn't you run away?" Their high spirits had chased them all the way to the reservoir. It was passingly cool beneath a ragged clump of bluegums but the truth was they didn't know where else to go. Sip looked at her shyly and smiled again as he'd been smiling on and off for most of the last half hour, on and off, like a Christmas light. His love for Ruthie, that for so long had formed the steady glow before which he warmed his cold and hungry life, flashed out with a hard bright intensity. He could hardly bear to look at her and only just managed these glances from beneath his lashes.

"Well," said Ruthie, "and didn't you hear me yelling? I yelled my lungs out, man." But she felt embarrassed whenever she thought about the woman and what she'd called Sip. The word *picannin* lurched between them: little black baby with crusty eyes and a hunger-sprung belly. "Oh, Dot," she said suddenly, "Dot, my love, come save me!" Had the woman really said that? Surely not. Sip began to laugh. "Oh, Dot," Ruthie said again, making her voice come out high and squeaky and grabbing at hanks of her hair and turning her head this way and that as if searching in vain for the stalwart who might recover her, "Oh Dot, my love, my lo-o-ove, come and save me from the terrible girl, come and lick my dirty toes and squeeze my hairy bum and, and—"

Sip was screaming with laughter now, rolling in the dirt and holding his stomach, and his cheeks were wet with mirth. Ruthie regarded him kindly. Shame, the poor kid was such a scrawny thing.

After a time Ruthie fell into a reverie and swiftly forgot about Sip, whom she had so casually rescued then abandoned to his laughter.

But Sip had stopped laughing. It was the water reservoir, its rusty, sun-stealing bulk that today seemed to creak in the wind although not a breeze stirred the leaves of the bluegums. The place held a terror for him that was as real as his fear of the water and as illusory as his sudden start at the bits of sun and shade that tore themselves to rag at his feet. Sometimes folks fell into the water tank, Sip knew—no one important, just vagrants and daredevils. Kids nobody wanted enough to shut them indoors at night. Although, Ruthie said, how could you?

Once last summer or the one before, Ruthie and he had hidden in the bushes and watched as the police fished out the bloated green stink of what one of these kids had become after a week in the tank. The smell!—it was like nothing he'd ever . . . rotten and sweet and guttery and it didn't float away in the air like other smells but hammered its way through his nose and into his brain and down his throat, and by the time the police had fitted the harness around the leaking, sagging, half-risen thing in the water and painfully winched it up, the smell had squeezed the fist of his stomach open and closed and he was doubled over and vomiting in the dust beneath the bushes.

This was long ago. Last year, at least. But Sip remembered looking over at Ruthie. Man, was he embarrassed. Yoh weh! She was sitting with her legs drawn up and her chin on her knees and she'd shifted a little away from him as was her nature, fastidious. And she was staring out at the reservoir, at the giant water tank with its slimy, rusted sides and at the policemen in their shirtsleeves, cursing and slipping on the narrow ledge. They'd wrestled all that was left of that terrible green kid from the water and now they were trying to lever it over the side but they were having the devil of a time, anybody could see that.

"Body's taken up too much water," one of the sergeants yelled out. "Bloody sponge!"

Ruthie had begun to bite her knee. Slowly and without taking her eyes off the scene before her she gnawed at the shiny tight skin of her kneecap. Oh, thought Sip, because he'd seen her bite this bite before, and how she wouldn't stop agitating at her knee (or the skin of her wrist or the inside of her elbow) until the blood began to run and then she'd take a deep breath and grow calm. Calmer.

The sergeant had clambered down the iron ladder and was yelling to the policemen on the top. He was shouting something and chopping the air in half with his hands. The stink was all around them. It was not a cloud, it was a gun to the head. The year had turned on its axis; it was no longer summer and Sip was cold beneath his bush. And the day, too, had turned around and was hastening towards the long shadows of late afternoon. Even the crickets in the veld had fallen silent as if to ask, *And now? So what? Who cares?*

The policemen had attached the harness and the slings and they were lowering the body down and trying to be careful, but try as they might and even though the sergeant on the ground was hollering at them and cursing them to hell and gone, they kept banging that poor green used-to-be against the sides of the tank. And what Sip remembered best from that day—better than the coldness under the bush or Ruthie pulling the blood out of her knee or the sound of the crickets starting up again, quite suddenly and all at once, when the last police van had trundled off down the dirt road (although it seemed he remembered all these things too and pretty well)—what Sip remembered best was the soft *plump-thump, plump-thump* of the body as at last it

Nightwatching

began its descent down the outside wall of the water tank and every few seconds or so hit the side.

It was a soft, intimate sound. Like a small, ripe melon— a musk or a honeydew—breaking open under pressure. *Plump-thump, plump-thump.* The sergeant down below cursing a blue streak and the policemen sweating above with their ropes and their harnesses, shouting "Gently, man," and "Hekelemanzi," and in between the lolling, terrible swollen thing bursting out of its straps and pouring with greasy water and every now and then banging against the reservoir tank and then the curses and the shouts would fade away and there would be only this sound, this overripe burst of melon flesh against the hard, cold walls of his imagination.

Well, okay. Sip shook his head hard as he'd trained himself to do and the past broke up into tiny pieces, the bright, colourful mosaics of incredulity and dispassion. Why, it had nothing to do with him!

He'd scarcely experienced this thought when Ruthie at his side sprang up as if the force of his reverie had somehow infected her, as if she too was remembering that day. "What now?" she yelled.

Sip stared at her warily. There was no telling with Ruthie. Was she angry or was she trying to calm herself by shrugging the anger from her shoulders like an ill-fitting sweater? He lowered his eyes and watched an ant stumble through the stubble grass—for how many minutes? Seconds, was all.

"Here," said Ruthie suddenly. She had remembered the marbles in her pocket and all but thrust them in two handfuls at Sip. "Now be careful and don't give them back to Dion this time, you hear?"

Confounded and dubious, Sip took the marbles from her and tied them carefully in his handkerchief. They made a heavy, knobbly bundle and dragged down the pocket of his ragged shorts until they gaped. But, so? With each step he took he clicked and clacked like a counting machine—four five *six*, six seven *eight*—and he tried to keep his gait slow and steady so as to preserve the threadbare lining of his pocket.

But presently he was forced to dig the bundle of marbles from his pocket and hold them before him as, arms pumping, heels lifting high, he began to stumble, then jog, then run after the bicycle that took off on the path before him. *Oh, Ruthie*, he almost but at the last moment did not call out, *Wait for me. Oh, Ruthie, my love, my love.*

Afterwards Ruthie couldn't believe how close she'd come to missing having dinner with them. There were no good restaurants, her dad was explaining, not like in Bloemfontein, so he'd arranged for Miriam to cook supper. But we can go out dancing afterwards, he promised Lena, there was quite

Nightwatching

a good place in town. "You too, Syl," he laughed, clapping the other man on the back. "In fact, now that I think about it, why don't I go and make that phone call I was telling you about. Rustle up some of the local talent."

"Sounds good, Lionel. You rustle 'em up and I'll take 'em dancing." Syl threw himself down on the sofa and winked at Ruthie.

The three of them had come home only minutes earlier, a rumble of gravel in the driveway, a spurt of laughter in the hall. Ruthie had come running in from the kitchen where she'd been nagging Miriam about the lamb chops. Miriam was good at lamb chops and her dad had said to grill them for supper with pepper and mint sauce, so that was all right, but eight, would eight be enough? Surely not.

"Three each for the men and two for your father's friend," Miriam explained yet again. "I told you already, women don't eat so much. And not that one, that one is always on diet, that I can tell you."

"And me?" Ruthie almost wailed. "What about my lamb chops?"

"Tcha, since when do you eat with the grown-ups, meisie?"

It was true, whenever her dad invited one of the commercial travellers over for supper Ruthie would eat with Miriam in the kitchen, the two of them listening to the radio and helping themselves from the stove or dealing Spite and Malice between helpings of the pap with gravy that Miriam always made no matter what else she was required to serve. Why, even now, even today on this night of all nights, the battered old pot with its crusty lid sat puffing steam on the back burner and every now and then Miriam broke off whatever she was doing to stir the pap briskly with a wooden spoon. And after every stir she would knock the edge of the spoon on the rim of the pot, clamp down the lid and sigh to herself. *Uh*-huh. As if, thought Ruthie, in the whole world, in the entire house and throughout the shadowy reaches of the kitchen, there was not one thing of any importance to her but the contents of that one battered pot puffing out its stupid little life on the back burner.

"Come, my girl," she coaxed now, "who will keep old Miriam company tonight?"

Ruthie glared at her impassively, willing her to stare her own foolishness in the face, for did she not eat supper with her father on nights when there was no company, which was every *other* night in the world practically, and she had never heard Miriam complain before. No, not once. On such nights Miriam sat outside in the courtyard if it was warm enough or else took her dinner plate into her room, and she often had company in the form of Sip, and even Sip's father, the gardener, who would occasionally sober up and come next door for a plate of something hot. This was the first time she'd ever heard Miriam complain of loneliness and Ruthie was monstrously suspicious, and angry too, yet with each second that passed the possibility of another lamb chop being taken out of the fridge and put on the grill seemed to be passing her by.

"Oh, please," Ruthie whispered to herself, plucking at the thin stuff of the clean white blouse she'd changed into after she had returned from the park. And she'd washed her hands and her face too and damped down her fringe until it lay flat against her high forehead. She had almost despaired of finding something to wear with the blouse, because she had nothing but the denim shorts she stood up in and an old pair of jeans and she discarded both as being too everyday and not at all suitable for the dinner that all day had gleamed and rustled and shimmered at the corners of her imagination. If only her dad would rouse himself to notice that she'd shot up two inches and in all directions over the summer. Nothing fit her anymore though she pulled and tugged at hems and armholes and necklines with no elastic in them, though she tucked herself in and held her breath and hunched her shoulders around the small tight buds of her breasts. All around her room she had flung these castoffs: T-shirts she could no longer pull over her head, skirts that hiked too far above her knees, dresses that wouldn't quite close in front. In a fit of pique she'd even ripped the bright pink party dress that her father had bought her in the spring from Kurtz Fashions. Now it lay at the foot of her narrow child's bed, spoiled forever but still bright as the colour of sucked Valentine's hearts, for it had only been worn once and it had never been washed at all.

Finally she noticed, at the back of her wardrobe, a skirt that an aunt from Johannesburg had sent. Her older cousin had outgrown the garment and could young Ruthven perhaps make use of it? This aunt had been in the habit of sending these small clothing parcels to the Blackburn family at regular intervals, wrapping up her maternal feeling for her poor sister's daughter in the outward layers of thrift and charitable obligation, but since Lionel Blackburn resented the first impulse and scorned the second, these parcels were never acknowledged and the aunt soon grew weary of eliciting nothing but her brother-in-law's ingratitude. For a time the aunt continued to phone the Blackburns once a year on Ruthie's birthday, which was also—as she never failed to point out—the anniversary of her poor sister's death, but in time even these dismal *memento mori* ceased and Ruthie had clean forgotten the existence of the aunt by the time she noticed the skirt. Well, maybe?

It was red, an unaccustomed colour in the denim blues and khaki drabs of her everyday wardrobe, but it fit and quite severely too, with a tightness about the hips that Ruthie was unused to and that made her feel twitchy and unpredictable. The hem had come undone on one side but that was nothing, nothing at all, and Ruthie tacked it up again with masking tape and a safety pin she rifled from amongst the notions in Sip's sewing kit. As for the white blouse it was crisp and clean for once but slightly too tight across the chest, the second button gaping and pulling; there was no getting away from it. But what if she were to leave the first two buttons open? She gazed at herself in the wavering glass of her dressing table and felt suddenly solemn with the weight of her newly spruced self. Why, she looked three years older, at least. Five, if you counted the white sandals she planned to wear. They were too small for her but she knew she would rather hobble through the evening than go down to dinner in her canvas tennis shoes.

"Yoh weh!" Miriam had gasped when she first saw her. "And who is this grown-up somebody come to help me set the table?" But then Miriam had handed her three place settings instead of four and the wrangling began in earnest.

"Oh, Miri, *please* put just one extra lamb on the grill and then if he says I can eat with them it'll be ready. Don't you see? That way it'll be ready. And if he says not, I'll eat it anyway, so either way—and I won't say a *word* and I'll help you wash up and, and, Miri, I'm sorry I called you a Bantu and tomorrow I'll teach you to play 'Chopsticks' if you like. It's easy and I'm a good teacher, you saw how I taught Sip just one two three, like that. Only, Miri? Can you take the cutlet out now, *right* now?"

Clucking, shaking her head, Miriam had put another lamb chop on the grill but she'd refused to let Ruthie set an extra place at the table or slide another bottle of Coca-Cola in the refrigerator or even draw one of the tall dining room chairs that stood about the edges of the room when not in use up to the dark mahogany rectitude of the dining room table. Ruthie stood to one side and studied the table through half-closed lids: the white cloth with its cross-stitching in "autumn" colours that her mama had sewn during the harsh winter months of her only pregnancy, the wide-brimmed soup bowls and heavy cutlery. On every side dish Miriam had placed a starched white napkin and Ruthie seized each of these napkins and began to fold them into closed fans and thread them through the prongs of the dinner forks.

When she had completed her three napkin fans and spread them out to her satisfaction she stood back once more and thought softly to herself as she had so often thought all that summer, *Oh, I wish . . . I want . . .* But what did she wish, what did she want? Was it to sit with the grown-ups and eat a lamb chop off the thick white dinner service? Yes, and have a napkin fan of her own, that too, and a water glass set a little to the right of her own wide-brimmed soup bowl. But that wasn't all or even mostly, or maybe it wasn't what she wanted at all. As always Ruthie grew beguiled by the words, lulled by their soft lapping plaint, *I wish . . . I want . . .*

The light from the setting sun slanted in through the dining room windows. It was the only gentle light that had fallen all day and the lace curtains caught it up and spread it in a pretty drifting pattern across the white cloth. Here and there the bowl of a wineglass glowed as if trembling with wine and the knives and forks cast small reflective gleams on the ceiling. The high, silver, wordless note of her desire rang through her like a tuning fork and Ruthie felt small suddenly, and suddenly lonely. She wished she could climb under the table and hide there, her chin on her knees, the salty flesh of her wrist caught between her teeth. She pressed her hands against the thin cotton of her blouse as if trying to smooth out the little bumps that had begun to swell beneath her skin. *Pat pat,* but it was no use, nothing would flatten the yeast of what rose in her like anticipation.

Miriam was standing at the hot plate fussing over her pot of soup. She could only manage one kind with any distinction, which was tiresome so far as Ruthie was concerned, but her dad always laughed and said tomato soup was the best kind of soup, it had few pretensions, indeed hardly any. In fact, now that he came to think of it, none at all.

A tomato was a tomato, a vegetable for all seasons, and the soup it produced was a fine and truthful soup. So that was that, winter or summer, tomato soup, tomato soup, tomato soup, and when company came a bit of sour cream on the top with parsley and chives. But now, watching Miriam stir and taste, squinching up her eyes as she always did with the tomato as if to stiffen her resolve against the acidity or the heat, a sudden pang assailed Ruthie. Would there be enough for her? Had Miriam, from the tins of paste and diced tomatoes and stock that still stood haphazardly about the kitchen counters, produced enough of the thin orangey broth to fill not merely three but all four of the wide-brimmed soup bowls that were the last remaining of her mama's trousseau?

The bowls were lovely, everyone said so, cream-coloured with a delicate gold filigree worked in a band upon their broad old-fashioned brims. But they were deep too, and seemed to swallow the very broth that filled them so that when ladled with soup to an acceptable level it was astonishing how swiftly the pot on the hot plate drained to a mere trickle, to nothing really.

"Oh, Miri," Ruthie burst out, hopping from one foot to the other in her agitation, "but will there be enough for me?"

Luckily the sound of the guests could be heard distinctly now, because the little red sports car had roared up to the house and the woman called Lena was laughing—was

Nightwatching

she always at the beginning or in the middle or at the end of a laugh?—Lena was laughing and saying, "No, boet, man, don't you dare! I swear if you so much as whisper a word of that terrible story—"

"Why, what'll you do to me, sis?" The brother had the sister's hands clasped together at the wrist and was holding a gold cigarette lighter high above her head. Every now and then she gathered herself together and leapt for it but she was weak with the giggles and eventually just gave up and collapsed in a heap on the sofa. "Here you go, sis," the brother teased and threw the gold lighter into her lap.

"Jirre! You two!" said Lena. She had propped her feet on the sofa and was rolling her beautiful dark eyes between her brother and Ruthie's dad. "You two boys are enough to wear a girl out, I tell you. Okay, who wants to make little Lena something cold to drink now, hmm? And not Coca-Cola either, Mr. Blackburn, I'm warning you."

Laughing, rubbing his hand across his forehead as he did when he was mildly perplexed, her dad went to the drinks cabinet and began rattling bottles about. "Campari and soda?" he called out.

"Mmm, lovely."

"And for you, Syl?"

"Soda, no Campari. With Scotch instead if you've got it. Hell, wait. No soda either."

The brother had a quick hard laugh that was no sooner begun than it was over, but Lena's laughter went on and on like the tinkle of her gold charms as they bobbed and shone at her wrist. "Coming, folks, coming right up," her father called from the drinks cabinet and poked his head into the kitchen to tell Miriam to fill up the ice bucket. Should she ask him now, should she? Ruthie was in a paroxysm of excitement and could hardly stand still with nerves. "Oh, please," she whispered again and pressed at the thin cotton that covered her chest. She fiddled at the button she'd left undone because it gaped, and then, losing courage, had hastily fastened again before coming downstairs. But all the indecision had loosened the threads that held the little button in place and now it threatened to come off in her hands.

If I don't look down, she thought, if I don't — But when she jerked her chin resolutely up, her eyes collided with the brother's eyes, with Syl's eyes, and he was laughing again, laughing those sharp barks, ha ha *ha*, and then he patted the sofa beside him as if to say, *What have we here?* And then Lena was turning around with big eyes and wondering, "Oh, lovely, isn't the child pretty, and is she going to join us for dinner?" And by the time her dad looked up with his mouth half open as if to say, *Well where did you get that red skirt from, my girl?* it was all more or less settled.

"Quickly, Miriam, one more place setting," said Ruthie,

hurrying into the kitchen. And she didn't say *I told you so* but really if some people would just mind their own business in the way of who was eating with whom then the world would be a much more pleasant place and also—here she busied herself with threading a napkin fan through the fork at her bread plate—and also she just hoped that old Miriam had listened to her about lamb chops and tomato soup, that she truly hoped. But Miriam just shrugged and laughed and carried on slicing the carrots for the French salad. She never bore a grudge or cared how wrong she had been or quarrelled with fate, not a bit of it. What was done was done—why fuss or feud? That was her motto, and it astonished Ruthie, truly it did, that one minute she could be so stubborn that not even a Free State mule on a sand road could wait her out and the next she was just plain old Miri, chopping her carrots and yawning.

The carrots! she thought suddenly. Surely they were sliced too thickly to suit the elegance of the salad for which they were destined. And the tomatoes—now that she looked closely—were pale wedges the colour of unhealthy gums and the lettuce was raggedy and noticeably damp. Her heart smote her, but what could she do? Oh, Miri, she mourned, and had half a mind to begin an argument, yet *another* one, but a burst of laughter from the lounge attracted her attention and the salad was, in any case, a lost cause.

Her dad was just returning from his phone call when she sidled into the lounge. "Yup, yup, looks like the Nordje girl can join us later on. Good family, nice girl. I think you'll get a kick out of her, Syl—both of you." Her dad was rubbing his hands together and not meeting her eyes. "All right, everybody sorted then? More drinks already? And then we must adjourn to the dining room because Miriam is ready to dish up and chez Blackburn tomato soup waits for no man."

"But, Lionel luvvy, surely we don't need to rush from one thing to another like headless chickens? Haven't we just got in, soentjie? Come on, you tell him, Ruthie, you tell him that your poor Auntie Lena just needs to sit here on the sofa with her feet up for a sec-y."

"That's right, Ruthie girl, you tell your old man to slow down. Does he always kick up the dust like this or have I forgotten what it's like to live in the big city?" Syl threw back his head and laughed. He beckoned Ruthie to sit beside him and she moved forward, but slowly, trying not to gaze at his soft, full lips and the small precise line of his moustache that grew with such intimacy above them.

"And what mischief did you get up to today, young lady? Out with the boys, was it? Now tell me, how many boyfriends are you stringing along, my girl? Tell your Uncle Syl, hmm."

It was extraordinary. She'd never heard anything like it. But even as she marvelled at his words she could feel the terrible blush beginning, the roar of the blood in her ears and then the heat that hummed up from under her arms to the back of her neck and across her forehead and over her chest and her cheeks. There was nothing she could do, a burning, blazing red girl lived inside her and a couple of unexpected words or a stranger's laugh might lure her out. Ruthie stared at the carpet and bit her lip and suffered.

"Well—" her dad began uncertainly, but Lena interrupted him.

"Ag, Syl, look what you've done now! The poor girl. No, man, really, nobody wants to hear your nonsense. Here, liefie, come sit here by your Auntie Lena and let's ignore him together."

Ruthie suddenly found herself pulled across the sofa and settled beneath Lena's proprietary arm. The unfamiliar contact was slightly shocking, because wariness was second nature to Ruthie. Like a cat she'd grown accustomed to keeping her distance. But, undaunted, Lena continued to enumerate the various ways in which the two of them could continue to ignore her clumsy boet. "Shame, he doesn't mean any harm, but," she finished off, taking a deep draw from her cigarette.

Now her dad was shaking his head and laughing and trying to usher them all to the table and Lena was saying, "No, but really I must just go and freshen up, *darling*."

Everything she said sounded playful and contradictory at the same time, as if she were a wayward child but also everybody's mother. *Oh, children, children!* she seemed always to be exclaiming, but was she hailing them as playmates or scolding them ever so slightly for their naughty ways? So then there was a whole bit of time where her dad and Syl talked about business and politics and her dad asked Syl if he was a card player and every now and then looked at his watch and worried about Miriam's tomato soup. Yes, said Syl, he was a demon for contract bridge and was there any chance of a game this weekend? And then, finally, Lena was back, standing in the doorway and saying, "All right, my treasures, what are we waiting for?"

Well, Ruthie could have told her what they were waiting for, of course, had been waiting for for fifteen minutes already and they would be lucky if the lamb chops were still edible by this time and not burnt down to charcoal, but the loveliness of Lena framed in the doorway, one hand on her throat to finger her necklace, quite took her voice away. She had changed and was wearing a pale gold party dress with thin spaghetti straps over her tanned shoulders. She'd twisted her hair up into two gold combs at the top of her head, but little curls still fell down and around her temples and ears and nape. On her feet was a pair of gold strappy sandals and then the charm bracelet, also gold. And there was one more gold thing, which

Nightwatching

was the necklace itself made of wide interlocking links that lay flat against the loveliness of Lena's throat where, in the hollow, her hand still twisted at the gold words that hung one above the other: *Live Love Laugh*.

Oh, thought Ruthie, oh.

She was the most beautiful sight that Ruthie had ever seen, all the pale and bright golds of her, all the brown firm flesh. There was the same sunny, smoky, perfume and cigarette, Sen-Sen and baby powder smell that Ruthie remembered from that morning. As she came forward into the room she tripped on the threshold and both men rose instinctively to catch her. "Ag, it's nothing," she chided, and instead took each by the arm and proceeded like a queen to the dining room.

In something of a huff Miriam had already ladled a helping of tomato soup into each of the wide-brimmed, gold-filigreed soup bowls. She was not one to tap her heels in the kitchen while the master of the house dawdled and blew smoke at the ceiling.

"Well now," said Syl, "I take it this is the famous soup de la maison." He lifted a brimming spoonful to his mouth and smacked his lips with gusto.

Lena giggled. "I hope she didn't poison it, that ousie in the kitchen. Did you see how she looked at me just now? Bloody cheek, like I'm gum on the bottom of her shoe or something."

Miriam had come in while Lena was still talking, to plonk down her French salad and hand around the side dishes of cream and chives. Ruthie stole a glance at her face but it was impassively un-Miriam-like, a closed book.

"Did I tell you that the Nordje girls are home from college?" her dad began hastily, and she tried to help him out by asking "Both?" although she knew, everyone did, that where one went the other followed, they were like twins although they were a full twelve months apart and the joke in the town was that they would never marry except a pair of brothers and always live but two metres apart. Tina and Trudy Nordje—one had blue eyes and one had brown but in all other particulars there was a reassuring sameness to the girls and Ruthie couldn't imagine one without the other. Her dad was telling Syl all about the Nordje girl he'd soon meet—but which one?—and Syl was grinning with all his teeth and Lena kept saying, "No *hon*estly, boet, you're not to wolf her down like that!" And presently Miriam banged the lid of the pot down hard in the kitchen to say, *Are you good and damn ready for your lamb chops now or what?*

So Ruthie helped take off the soup dishes, careful to keep her thumb out of the bowls, and then stood by the side of the stove as Miriam dished up each plate with its grilled lamb chops, spoonful of rice and little heap of boiled pumpkin with butter. She always helped when there was company

Nightwatching

and tonight was no different even though she was one of the company. "Thank you, Ruthie," her dad said when everyone was served and she finally took her seat, and he winked at her, a surprising thing, a secret pact.

"Ruthie, tell your Auntie . . . your Auntie Lena—" But Lena couldn't seem to finish her sentence. She'd gotten the giggles and they bubbled from her, bright and iridescent. Each time she began again, gamely enough, and each time she dissolved anew into little spumes and runnels and fountains of mirth. The problem, it seemed, was the lamb chop.

"Oh, don't mind her," said Syl. "Campari gives her the giggles."

"No, it's the chop, it's the chop." Lena was weak with laughter. She leaned her head against her arm and gestured. "It's so small—I've never seen such a small piece of meat. And dry, too. Listen, Lionel, that girl of yours is a terrible cook, terrible. Now here's what I'm going to do, skat—after supper I'm going into that kitchen and show her how to grill a cutlet. Do you a favour, man, and meantime, meantime—" Lena dissolved in giggles again, laughing so hard that she began to hiccup.

"There you go, old girl, there you go," said Syl kindly, and poured her a glass of water. He turned to Ruthie's dad. "Personally I like my chop on the well-done side, Lionel old fellow. But my little sister here has always had a penchant for rarity. She likes to see the blood run. So—no, ja—we must try to keep her out of the kitchen."

All the grown-ups were laughing now, but Ruthie only watched Lena as she sat between the two men, all pale and bright golds and sudden hitches of laughter and one hand playing with the links about her neck so that the light kept flashing onto one word and then another: *Live Love Laugh*. She felt sad for Miriam stuck in her lonely kitchen and the object of such fun-poking and merriment, but angry at her too for how far she had fallen in the estimation of others. The world wobbled on its strange Saturday night kilter and Ruthie put out a hand to steady herself, because Miriam was a stranger to her now. Such moments were rare but terrible—those times when the cozy, yolky "we" of Miriam and Ruthie separated out into two people, neither of whom she recognized.

"Oh, Miri," she whispered, concentrating hard. But it was no use, she'd lost the knack, and the sound of the other woman's name, for once, rang hollow, did not reassure, was not a talisman or a comfort or a cure.

A strange thing had happened, a strange series of events she should say, so strange that Ruthie could barely credit it, but nothing else would explain the outcome: Syl was taking her

Nightwatching

to the drive-in and afterwards to the Casablanca Roadhouse off Ontdekkers Road. She'd gone up to her room to brush her hair and was staring at herself in the wavy glass of her dressing table mirror thinking, *Oh, but how?*

First the phone call had come in the middle of coffee to say that the Nordje girl—Tina or Trudy—had taken ill and must beg off the evening. Not to worry, her dad had said looking worried, easy enough to find someone else. But it had not been easy. It had been quite impossible, in fact. "Ag, this town!" her dad had exclaimed coming back from the phone yet again, his forehead wrinkled. "But boet can come with us," said Lena, stretching out her arms in that way she had, linking herself between the two men. "Certainly not," Syl laughed, "I'm nobody's third wheel, sis." "Well, we must all just stay home together," her dad said, "make a bit of an evening of it." But Syl said absolutely not and he wouldn't hear of it, and "My God, are you trying to embarrass me, man? No, no, you two kids get the hell on out of here. I'll take the opportunity to catch up on my newspaper reading or my beauty sleep or whatever. Ruthie will take care of me—won't you," he said, and wiggled his pinkie finger at her.

So that was that. Goodbye and good luck. Her dad was in the middle of telling her when to go to bed, which was perhaps the strangest thing about the evening so far because he'd never seemed to care when she went to bed or what she did when she got there—"Straight to bed and *no* reading," he was just in the middle of saying—when Lena said, "Lionel, leave the poor kid alone, you old mother hen," and pulled him round to look at her. Oh, but she did look beautiful, thought Ruthie, surely the most beautiful thing she'd ever seen, all ready to go dancing with a gold clutch bag in her hand and a sort of silvery shine to her long narrow eyelids.

But that was only the beginning of the strange thing that had happened, the middle of which was that almost the minute the door slammed shut behind her dad and Lena, Syl had grabbed her by the hand and said, "Okay, my lovely, what's the game plan?" Miriam had long ago departed, yawning, to her own room and Ruthie couldn't think what young people did on a Saturday night, and she certainly wasn't going to have Syl follow her around to her usual haunts. The thought of him hidden in the shrubbery on Bleeker Street or in the tall grass beneath the Benders' bedroom window!

The movies, he hazarded, the discotheque, the drive-in? Oh, that's a good idea, had she ever been to the drive-in? Never! What a tragedy. (A *trag*edy, she mouthed. The word was crisp and granular on her tongue, like a sugar cube.) "Run upstairs and get ready, my lovely, your carriage awaits."

Ruthie stirred herself and the dim reflection in the mirror moved with her. It was so dark in the room that she could barely see herself anymore. She had damped her fringe down for the last time and pinched her cheeks to get the blood up in them and rubbed Vaseline on her lips to make them shine. She was so glad of the red skirt, so purely glad, though she had somehow gone ahead and lost the small plastic button on her white cotton blouse and her sandals were too small, which made her insteps ache with every damn step she took. Should she go ahead and change? She gazed at her reflection in the dim glass of the three-way mirror as if to make out the answer there, but it was no use. And besides. She pressed her palms slowly to her chest, then whirled around and ran downstairs.

Syl was waiting for her in the red sports car. "Oho," he said when he saw her, "jump in, my lovely, and away we go." So she was to be *my lovely*, was she? Okay. "Now that was a marvellous dinner," he said as he turned into the service road. "Quite marvellous. Do you dine like that every night or just when there are guests?"

She couldn't be certain if he was laughing at her or at Miriam or at her dad, she just could not be certain. But when she darted a glance at him she saw that he had already forgotten his question and was drumming out a little tune on the steering wheel, da dada *da*, and peering out into the dusk, because there were no street lights until the turnoff to Ontdekkers. She'd only ever driven in a couple of cars before: her dad's bottle-green Valiant and Mr. Feinstein's maroon Pontiac, and both cars were great clunky boats that spread across the road, solemnly ticking up the miles per hour while guzzling gas (her dad's words) and depreciating their value (Mr. Feinstein's). And in both these cars she'd bounced about mostly in the back seat, feeling her bones jolt in their sockets with every bump and divot in the road. But the red sports car was a different animal entirely.

It was low-riding and compact and the wheels seemed constructed of a thicker rubber than the wheels of any other car that Ruthie had ever driven in. She could barely feel the road beneath her, neither the gravel of the service road nor the macadam of Ontdekkers, onto which they were, even now, turning. And the leather of the seats was soft and tan-coloured and cushiony and she hung suspended and slightly canted between the road and the sky, flashes of which passed overhead through the roof vent. The stars were coming out well enough and a moon, small and red on the horizon. Nobody, no one, nowhere, she thought, aiming herself down the middle of the road, straight down the middle where the cat's eyes glinted their nervous green light.

They didn't talk because of the wind crashing in through the roof vent and filling the car with a loud hummy noise—but also what was there to say? Ruthie wondered. She was glad of the wind even though it whipped her hair about her

Nightwatching

head, hither and yon, and caused a fine grit to fly about the car. Her eyes watered but it was not tears, just the wind and the speed, the grit that flew up off the road and the residue of the hot day on the cooling tarmac. "Nobody, no one, nowhere," she whispered but in a different key, a tender mood this time as if to say, *Little one, little one, don't take on so.* Her father had spoken to her in this manner once or twice, long ago, when he'd thought to comfort her, but for what she could not now remember. Well, what of it? It had been a long time ago, the remembered slight and the words of comfort. *Little one, don't take on so, don't take on so.*

Something, some small veld animal, dashed across the road and Ruthie stiffened against the back of her seat in preparation for Syl's wild skid and weave to avoid the creature. But he did no such thing; his hands on the wheel were steady, as was his foot on the accelerator, and he smiled serenely into the distance. "Can't slow down on the highway," he said when he caught her staring at him. There'd been a bump to the rear of the car but it could have been any old thing. Still, she couldn't stop staring at his well-cut profile.

"Can't slow down at this speed," he explained again. "Might cause an accident."

A silence thundered down into the car and at the same time the wind dropped away and Ruthie was suddenly aware of the cologne Syl used. He'd slid the roof vent shut and was still drumming out his tune on the steering wheel—da dada *da*—but with the other hand he'd managed to light a Peter Stuyvesant, Your International Passport to Smoking Pleasure, and was lifting it to his mouth. "Looks like we're nearly there," he said, pointing with his cigarette to the sign that said WELCOME TO THE TOP STAR! CHILDREN TEN AND UNDER FREE! "And how old are you, my lovely?"

But when she said eleven going on twelve he frowned and said, "Let's try a little something, shall we?" And what it was, was that she must hunch down in the seat next to him with a blanket over her and pretend to be ten. "All right, sport?" Okay, then. She didn't mind. She didn't really mind. She was ten once so she'd had the practice of it, and when the woman at the wicket said "And how old is your daughter?" she knew enough to keep still. "Ten years old, ma'am," he said, although she expected him to say, *She's not my daughter.* "One adult then," said the woman with a big smile and he smiled right back at her, but when the car peeled away from the wicket he said, "Silly cow, we pulled one over on her though, didn't we?"

The first two squawk boxes they tried were broken and the third jabbered uselessly but they finally found one whose sound synchronized with the bright images working out their shadow play on the giant screen before them. Ruthie was transfixed. A mouse chased a cat and then a

Nightwatching

cat turned around and chased a mouse right back and then there was also one about a coyote and some road runner—was it?—and some more cat and mouse and then an angry duck. Lisping. No, but it wasn't the cartoons, exactly, and the bright, lickable colours and the walloping music. It was, it was how everything she was and had been and would become was focused on that vivid, flickering screen so that for minutes at a time Ruthie seemed to lose all sense of reality and it was as if she were watching her own lost and lonely life played out in the dark. It was nothing like lying beneath the privet or crouching in the long grass and looking in at the neighbourhood windows for seconds at a time, little snatches of *who do you think you are?* Nothing like. Or, no—perhaps—but bigger. And with no risk of anyone staring back at her. Yes, that was the thing, no risk of anyone catching her out.

"Hey, you." Syl laughed. "Enjoying yourself?" His finger on her shoulder was a surprise, a good one. "Well, I can certainly see you're enjoying yourself!" The cartoons were over and there was a newsreel now, a cavalcade. They were opening two new mines on the reef but America was having a terrible time with the Communist threat. Syl laughed and said, "Oh boy, that old war!" He lit another cigarette and Ruthie could hardly believe it but the very next minute, right there on the screen, there was an advertisement for

{155}

the same brand of cigarettes. Peter Stuyvesant—*Wherever You Go . . . Peter Stuyvesant Is There!*

"Snap!" said Syl, holding up his box, but Ruthie could tell that it was nothing special to him. Probably things like that happened to him all the time, she thought. Wonders.

At intermission cars were hooting and some kids were playing on the swings. There were advertisements for Simba crisps and Eskimo Pie up on the big screen but these were stale, unmoving affairs with no jingle to them.

"Thirsty?" asked Syl.

Yes, no. She nodded then shook her head. She hardly knew what to do anymore. Thirsty—well, was she? No, it wasn't thirst but *like* thirst. And not hunger either, though very *like* hunger. What it was, was the winged flightless thing that she'd felt opening out in her when she was watching the cartoons and the newsreel and the advertisements but even before that, since the beginning of the summer. All summer this awkward clumsy thing had peered out of her eyes and lit on this object or that: Mrs. Bender's curved white shoulder under Mr. Bender's arm, some mother's voice in the dusk calling "Come inside, my luvvy," the blond boy in the park. And all summer long.

At night she'd come home tired from her watching, but still she couldn't sleep for the strange notched feeling. It was a longing feeling, as if peering into all these other homes had bred a homesickness in her. But this was absurd for she had a home, a place, a bed. Well, and if—? She'd learned, that summer, to touch herself down there in the dark; she had found a way to unbutton sleep. So, okay. But she did not think of her nighttime self during the day, she did not. There were these two girls and they did not meet in the middle, that was all. "Come inside, my luvvy," called the voice of the mother in the dusk and soon the park was empty of all the kids except for the disdainful blond boy who wouldn't give her the time of day.

Syl had returned from the drive-in concession with two bottles of Coca-Cola and a packet of Simba salt-and-vinegar crisps to share. And straws, which was fantastic because if there was one thing she loved better than drinking Coca-Cola it was drinking Coca-Cola straight from the bottle through a straw, which she almost never got to do.

"Whoa," he said with the first good pull, "sugar rush, baby." And he clasped the bridge of his nose tight. But she liked that feel of hard bubbles at the back of her head even if it made her sneeze, which she did and with gusto.

"Nuh-uh, too rich for my blood," said Syl, "good thing I've brought my own provisions." He took a couple of tin mugs from the back seat and tipped some Coca-Cola into one, then rustled around until he found something wrapped in brown paper but liquid inside because she could hear it gurgle. It had a screw-top and Syl unscrewed it carefully and poured off some of the liquid, stirring the mixture with his index finger.

"Want a taste?" he offered. But it was only brandy and Coke—she'd had it before because that's what the commercial travellers drank when they came over to play poker with her dad. She would take the dirty glasses back to the kitchen for Miriam and there would be quite a lot left over in some of those glasses.

"Wait, I'll make you some too," said Syl.

Bloody. Because then she had to hand over her bottle and he poured half into the other tin cup and some of the brandy from the screw-top bottle. He used her straw to mix the two together, then threw it out the window so it was goodbye hard bubbles too. Well, okay. All around them the other drivers were getting impatient, hooting their heads off and flashing their car lights unto kingdom come. Every now and then a searchlight would sweep through the massed cars on their rows of hummocks and pick out a bit of mischief—an adult helping a kid to urinate in the bushes or a couple of grappling teenagers. Each new indiscretion would set off a fresh volley of communal honking and flashing lights as if every member of the audience was of one voice, one mind, and that in the mind to be humoured, until finally—she'd never known the meaning of the word *bliss* until this moment but it was, it was *bliss*—the great whirring blue light behind the car park started up again.

She glanced sideways and in the pure blue light of her bliss she could make out Syl's profile and his arm flung sideways across the seat beside her. He was looking at the screen from over the top of his mug, but she looked away directly because she didn't want him to catch her looking at him. The movie began to be pretty good—just about the best she'd ever seen. There was a part where the janitor began to tell the little girl, the bad seed, what would happen to her when she went to jail and got electrocuted. There were pink electric chairs made especially for little girls, he said, and also blue ones for boys, and they were miniature-sized so as to fit these little boys and girls. But they killed just the same and with a terrible *ftzz-ftzz* sound as of meat frying. And from then on, whenever the janitor saw the little girl, he made this terrible sound—*ftzz-ftzz ftzz-ftzz*—laughing like a crazy thing.

Ruthie grinned in the dark. She was already planning how to tell this story to Sip, about the little blue electric chairs made especially for boys, bad little boys like him. *Oh, Sip*, she would say, *Sip my poor fellow, how would you like to have your very own custom-made chair?* And he would—but what would he do really? Nothing much, which was the problem with old Sip. Maybe widen his eyes, maybe hang his head.

But to please her, only to please her, or because he'd somehow divined that he had failed to please her.

The girl on the screen was looking at the janitor with a cold detached gaze. It was the kind of look that had so little warmth to it that the other person barely felt the look settle on him. There was no such look in real life, of course, only in the movies. In real life, as Ruthie very well knew, every look, every glance, every damn stinking stare had a weight to it. Not always heavy, not always a slap in the face or a punch in the stomach, true, but even a cat's paw against the cheek was enough to make a person look up. Well, she was a watcher; she knew about looking. Dion! she thought suddenly and out of nowhere, but once she'd thought of him she knew she'd found the right size boy to sit on her baby-blue electric chair. She grinned again and sipped from her tin mug, the drink much too sweet with the brandy added in, but oh well.

"What are you smiling at like that all by yourself in the dark?" asked Syl, gathering the thin cotton stuff of her sleeve in his fingers. "I've been watching you smiling all night like you have a secret," he whispered. He turned away from her but it was only to pour more brandy into her mug because the Coca-Cola was finished.

She was feeling sleepy so she put her head down on the back of the seat but he moved closer at the exact moment

Nightwatching

she did and so it turned out that she was resting her cheek on the palm of his hand, sort of, and he let two of his fingers drift down into the crook of her neck.

Oh, did he mean that? He couldn't have, she thought, and she lifted her head a bit to make it easier for him to shift his hand away.

"Settle down, silly," he said. "I'm not going to eat you! I only want to make you more comfortable."

It was true, though, lying with her hot cheek pressed against the cool palm of his hand was comfortable and it was comfortable, too, when he began to massage her neck lightly; she felt warm and drowsy but, no, also tight and a little bursty. Her breasts had begun to hurt again in that sort of pleasantly itchy way they did these days and she tried to stop herself from rubbing them. Then she tried to stop herself from even thinking about rubbing them because something had happened to Syl's fingers, which were getting very tingly and low down and kept dipping below the neck of her blouse and stroking at the top of her chest where the swells began—they were still only swells; she'd examined them and how often in her room with the door closed. Oh, how had his fingers heard what her mind was trying not to think?

"Oho, what have we here?" Syl whispered, and his breath was sweet and sticky with all the brandy and Coke he'd been drinking, but smoky too from the cigarettes. Now his hands were right down on the tops of her breasts and he was making her nipples stand up with his touching. The red girl who lived inside Ruthie and who engulfed her at the first sign of mortification began to stir.

"Relax, baby," said Syl, "you know you want to." The bad-seed girl on the screen was still looking her weightless looks and making her easy kills and it was all, all really quite *fas*cinating. She was a pretty good piano player too, which she must remember to tell that stupid, stinky Dion. Ruthie needed to wee really bad but she didn't want to say. He had another hand on her stomach, which was making it worse, the wanting to wee and the not knowing how to say. Red girl was lapping over her, red girl was thrumming through her blood and scorching her armpits but she really, she had to, she just . . .

"I have to go to the toilet," she burst out, trying to pull away.

"Not now," said Syl, breathing his sticky breath against her ear. "In a minute."

But didn't he know that it was very bad for the kidneys to wait even a minute longer than you had to? Miriam had said so and lots of other things along these lines and emphatically too. Suddenly and with all her might she longed for Miriam and then this moment, too, passed without a ripple into the end of her girlhood and was gone.

Nightwatching

He took his hand from her stomach and she felt a little eased. The girl in the movie liked to play a tune Ruthie seemed to recall from somewhere. Over and over she played this tune that knocked at the door of her memory. But the door remained stubbornly shut and anyway she had other things to worry about, because now Syl, who'd been using his free hand to rummage about in his pants, had brought out his thing and was trying to make her hold it.

She did not want to. She did not.

"Well, aren't you the little tease," he said.

Bad-seed girl had just set her sights on someone new to kill. She was no tease but meant every damn thing she did. Ruthie planned to become just like her one day, or someday soon, or whichever came first. Syl was pressing against her with his thing in his hand and his eyes closed. She thought suddenly that she would close her eyes too and then none of this would be happening. It didn't work and then it didn't work worse. Syl breathed with a horrible yellow breath into her neck and bad seed girl thumped out "*Au clair de la lune*" on her piano, over and over again. She knew she'd heard that tune somewhere before.

"Hnh-hnh-hnh?" panted Syl and spasmed himself quiet.

Ruthie rolled sideways and yanked at the door handle. The speaker that had been winched to her car window crashed to the gravel, still attached to its cord and squawking uselessly.

Ruthie was stricken. She didn't know where the toilets were and instead made a dash for the thin fringe of trees beyond the rows and rows of watching cars. When she got there she unrolled her panties and squatted, pissing into the ground as she had as a child on long car journeys when her father's hands had supported her under the armpits and when she was done he'd given her a little shake to end off with.

She stayed that way for a while crouching on the ground and looking up into the great humming blue light of the projector. And were all those glinting particles of dust and dream that hung suspended in its beam merely images on their way to becoming the movie that was still playing out its life on the giant screen behind her? For some reason she no longer cared to watch it; she kept her head carefully averted.

A fugitive breeze rustled up from nowhere special and cooled her aching forehead but did nothing much for her jumping stomach and her nerves and her feeling of throw-upiness, so presently she bent over again and did just that—threw up in the bushes. Wiped her mouth. Threw up again, wiped. Did she feel better? Did not, not especially. She found a clean bit of grass and lay down. From where she lay on her dark, rolling bit of earth the stars were doused, but the moon was somewhere out there, no longer red and horizon-bound but far away and looking as lame-dog lonely as she felt.

After another long time she felt about gingerly like

someone feeling for broken ribs, thinking *here? . . . here?* It was only words she was fumbling for, yet for once they seemed to come hesitantly, timorously, from long ago and far away. Out in the desert a great sphinx arose out of the burning sand, half-man, half-beast. His scorn and curl of cold command, his, his . . . "Ozymandias," she whispered. And then again, "Ozymandias! Ozymandias!" until it came at her in a rush. *I met a traveller from an antique land Who said: "Two vast and trunkless legs of stone Stand in the desert . . ."*

Gradually the words became a pulse to tame her wild flurry. Her breathing settled and her stomach, a little. *"My name is Ozymandias, king of kings: Look on my works, ye Mighty, and despair!"*

A man was coming through the bushes. Hissing her name like a lover. "Ruthie, you little bitch," he was calling softly, "you better come out now, or I swear to God I will find you and *when* I find you, so help me, you will wish you'd never met me."

She had to laugh. But she did not, she did not laugh. Instead she carried on doing her "Ozymandias" in her head.

"Ruthie," the man called again, but louder. "I'm counting to three. I'm counting to three, but you'd better be out by two, you little cunt, or I'm telling your daddy all about his sweet baby girl."

The cars near the windbreak began to flash their lights

because the man's voice had grown so loud and belligerent. "Hey, we're trying to watch a movie here, man!" someone yelled out of a car window and an empty bottle of beer crashed down nearby.

"Ru-u-u-thie," the man called in a soft wheedling tone. "Come on now, baby. No harm done. Let's just go home, okay, meisie. Come home with your Uncle Syl. Ru-u-u-thie! Ru-u-u-thie! Ru-u-u-thie!"

It was these long, drawn-out, sorrowful ululations of her name that decided her in the end, and just so that he'd be quiet and stop agitating her in this new way she got up from the ground and followed him to the car.

"Fuck, girl!" he said when he saw her in the light from the dash, and he tried clumsily to pull leaves from her hair and dust down her blouse but she winced so hard from him that he stopped in case she tried to run off into the night again, which she bloody would have, no question of it.

"Then fix yourself up, man." He indicated her hair, her earth-stained hands, her gaping blouse. In her headlong flight she had lost a shoe and jettisoned the other. Her skirt was twisted about her waist and there was a long and bloody scratch on one knee. But she was at a loss; she really did not know what to do. Slowly she reached into her hair and began to lift out the leaves and twigs that had been caught, making a little heap of them in the ashtray that stood ajar with a couple of stubbed-out cigarette butts inside. *Wherever You Go . . . Peter Stuyvesant Is There!*

"Oh, for chrissake!" He snapped a handkerchief from his pocket and spat on it. "Here," he said, shoving it at her. She must use it to clean her hands and face and effing get on with it.

Then he yanked on the ignition and peeled on out of there, and she took the handkerchief by the tips of her very fingers and tried to drop it behind the seat. No fucking way, his spit on her. But he caught her and grabbed the handkerchief back. Spat again.

"Here, girl, or do you want me to—?"

There was no food to come up though her stomach pitched about, no drink though her throat closed over, and the traveller had walked off into the desert and was not coming back though she called and called for him. She wiped her face and hands on the hanky then she stared down the long grey highway all the way home. Nobody, no one, nowhere. All the way home.

With a bad grace but an expertise born of long practice Miriam was preparing breakfast in the Sunday morning kitchen. No one was down yet except for Mr. Blackburn, spruce in yet another bright blue golf shirt that made him seem precise and attentive whilst throwing the kitchen and all its shadowy, slightly grimy edges into the blur of not-quite-wakefulness. He'd been drinking cup after cup of strong black coffee and now he was on his second bowl of porridge. He was capable enough for a man, Miriam thought, and on weekends could manage the coffee pot and the bowl of porridge on the stove. As for Ruthie, she'd long ago taught the child to make herself oatmeal, which had staying power, and for lunch sandwiches, and then she would come in again in the late afternoon to make supper. That's how she'd trained them, the Blackburns, and every Sunday since for how long she couldn't remember, she'd slept in a while, then gone to church, if she felt like singing, or to visit this one or that one, if she felt like walking, and always in the afternoon one or another of her children would visit, Jericho, Jonas or Temperance Thandile.

Mr. Blackburn coughed and rattled his newspaper. Ho, thought Miriam, am I making too much noise for Mr. Sunday Morning here? Well, he must just learn to lump it, the big blue baby! And she commenced to jostle her dishes in earnest, turning the heat up on the stove so that the butter in the pan hissed to mimic the anger she felt. But even as the butter bubbled and turned brown at the edges she felt her anger subside and she reached to turn off the burner. Jericho was away, she knew, although she did not know where he'd been sent by

Nightwatching

his movement or what his mission was, but she prayed God for his safety. Her valiant son. And Jonas would not come to visit this afternoon either, because he was studying for his final bookkeeping exams, and had been for two months now. He was her conscientious son. But Temperance Thandile, her daughter, her life, had sent word that she would come and Miriam's heart rejoiced her.

Hmm, condensed milk, sardines, white bread and apricot jam, Coca-Cola. Miriam ticked off Thandile's favourite foods, making a note of which ones she must still secure from Mr. Blackburn's pantry before tea time. Oh, and Hanepoot grapes.

From within the house the sounds of stirring could now be heard. A toilet flushed and a man's voice called, "Morning, sis, time to rise and shimmy." Miriam stared at Mr. Blackburn through the pages of his newspaper as if to say: *Look what you have done, you great blue baby—not only do you visit your fancy woman upon us but you must wish her silly, no-account brother too! And have me stand here making French toast for the lot of you on my morning off. Well, what do you have to say for yourself? Speak up!*

As if he could hear her every word, for Miriam was an expert at looks—she'd honed them to a precise and eloquent art—Mr. Blackburn hunched deeper into his newspaper. Coughed some, wriggled first this way and then that.

{169}

Then broke off his restlessness to stir his irritation, for some noisy minutes, into his coffee.

Uh-huh. Once she'd made her point and that point was well made, Miriam forgave him as suddenly as she had wordlessly upbraided him. That was just her way. With an easy heart she turned to the stove and began to break her eggs into the bowl, cutting thick slices of white bread and wondering, cinnamon and sugar? Or honey? There was a clatter in the hall and the fancy woman tripped in, *ac*tually tripped in, because of her high heels, and whoever heard of wearing high heels to breakfast? Miriam had to smile.

"Oopsa daisy," said Mr. Blackburn, catching her just before she fell, "and don't you look as fresh as one."

As a daisy, he meant. The Lena woman laughed gaily with a sound like a silver bell. Just exactly like a silver bell, thought Miriam, as if someone had once told her that her laughter sounded like bells ringing and now they must all listen to the silly tinkle every time something caught her fancy. Rolling her eyes, Miriam turned the heat up on the burner so that the butter bubbled and browned and the egg and milk mixture that she was pouring onto the thick slices of bread hissed fiercely, but, ah, nothing was loud enough to drown out the woman's tiresome ways, her whispery kisses and fluttery trills, and good Lord was she, was she trying to tickle Mr. Blackburn now? But surely not?

Nightwatching

"Mmph, ho, ah-*ha*," laughed Mr. Blackburn, sounding uncomfortable. No bells there.

Miriam gazed out the window resolutely, because she didn't want to see Mr. Blackburn being poked and prodded into reluctant merriment by the Lena woman. Tinkle, tinkle, tinkle went the silly silver bells and the French toast bubbled in the pan and burnt at the edges and Mr Blackburn cleared his throat the way he did when he had something important to say but all he said was "How's that fresh pot of coffee coming, Miriam?" Shaking her head sorrowfully, for how was it possible that a man should lose himself, and so entirely, forgetting everything that he'd been taught of Sunday morning self-reliance, Miriam piled the French toast onto a serving dish and put it before Mr. Blackburn, adding a jar of honey and another of jam to the array of breakfast condiments—butter, sugar, cinnamon—that jostled for space on the table.

Well, and now? Miriam looked at him kindly. Her indulgence had rendered her kind; she wiped her hands on her apron and, placing these same hands on her wide, firm hips, gazed down upon Mr. Blackburn fondly. Well, he was not so bad, a good father, a good employer; he had a reputation for honesty in the town and the mine boys who came to the Concession Store never got short shrift. As for the Lena woman, she'd seen it before, and how many times? Some cat came along, playing the kitten, with a silver bell around its neck and rubbing itself up and down on the nearest leg. *Tcha, humba wena!* she had a mind to say to this cat, but to the man she could not be stern, for what was a man but the result of the unequal contest between his resistance and his submission? The best put up a fight but, after all, what did such weak-willed fighting signify? And the worst?

Miriam turned away and resumed her window-gazing in earnest once more, for just such a worst had this very minute made his way into the kitchen and she had no interest at all in catching his ugly, pale-eyed glance. What had Ruthie called him? A dog panting after his supper. Well, the child certainly had a way with words and a feeling for despondency. But whether it was in Miriam to greet him or not, smile at him or not, incline her head in his direction or merely turn away, Lena's brother had already seated himself at the kitchen table and was spooning jam over two thick slices of French toast. And not offering the food to others, as was only proper, or choosing whether to eat or to speak but doing both and all at once and to ill effect.

"Well, folks," he said when he could speak again, "well, folks, and what's the program today?"

In the silence that followed, Miriam could hear Mr. Blackburn wondering what to say because, in truth, there was nothing to do in this town on a Sunday; nothing was open

Nightwatching

except for the Greek Caffy at noon and the petrol station out on the highway and the churches—every one of them from Our Lady of the Rosary to the three Dutch Reformed churches and every other church in between, Calvinist, Lutheran, Methodist, Pentecostal and Assembly of God. At ten o'clock the neighbourhood church bells rang out; it was an assault to the ears, Mr. Blackburn often said, clapping his hands over them. After that the Sunday quiet stretched out as long and unbroken as the highway out of town, this highway that Miriam often imagined running through all the little prairie towns of the Orange Free State, each one sunk in its separate air of Sunday lethargy or religious piety or just plain contrariness. Usually Mr. Blackburn took his time over the Sunday papers, setting aside the comics for Ruthie, then he would go about his weekly accounts, laying out his ring binders and Ledger on the green baize of the dining room table. In the afternoon a nap and in the evening a game of poker with any commercial travellers who might be in town, and so on and so forth, and with one thing and another a day might pass and usually did.

Miriam leaned her head on her hand and squinted up into the high blue sky. There were no clouds, but a slight breeze was rustling the kitchen curtains. Out beneath the privet hedge the bicycle was gone again and there were fresh tire marks in the red dirt. Was Ruthie out so early then?

She'd thought the child would be underfoot in the kitchen all morning, but Ruthie was a law unto herself and only predictable in her perversity. Sunday was always the hottest day of the week, a day sealed tight by sanctity, and already the heat outside was boiling up a good head of steam before roaring through the streets like a mad dog. Out in the veld the crickets were humming and the sound was a sort of involuntary mechanical description of the heat, at once empty and full of desolation but also and only just itself, just the uneven rhombus of road and veld and crazy blue sky that she walked out into every day as if into a version of her own life. *Hello, Miriam, well—hello.*

". . . And then, or maybe . . ." Mr. Blackburn was still trying to think of a Sunday program to please his guests but no one was listening to him. The Lena woman had stopped laughing her silvery bells and instead was giggling in great nose snorts in between which she kept saying, "No, Syl, but no, no, boet, nee man!" And this was because her brother was leaning over her, a square of toast still in one hand, but with the other he was tickling her, poking his fingers between her ribs and into her armpits and then ribs again. Lena began to snort more and more, and then to squeal in high breathless yips.

Ag really, thought Miriam, what *was* it with the du Toits and tickling. First Lena did Mr. Blackburn and then her brother did Lena, and if someone didn't stop him it looked like he was going to tickle the poor girl to death. Already she was holding herself, holding herself *down there*, and gasping, "No, boet, man, stop it, I have to go wee-wee."

"Oho, off you go, little girl, off you go. Don't want you to wet your panties," said the brother finally, pushing the square of toast into his mouth.

Miriam stole a look at Mr. Blackburn because she would bet he'd never heard such talk, never in his life, and Mr. Blackburn said, "The coffee, Miriam, the coffee for the *third* time, girl."

The kitchen went suddenly quiet or seemed to except for the wobble of the ceiling fan and the ticking of the red-faced kitchen clock with its nervous little second hand and the buzzing of the flies on the windowsills, but as to this last Miriam couldn't say whether the buzzing was inside her head or outside of it. Yoh, she thought, girl? And then again but louder, Girl? Lena was giggling but no one was tickling her and the brother was crunching at his toast as if this toast were a creature made of bones and not just bread, and bread soaked in egg at that. How did he do it? wondered Miriam as she took the coffee pot off the burner and set it on a trivet beside Mr. Blackburn.

Then she wiped her hands on her apron before untying this very apron and hanging it on the back of the door and closing this door behind her as she stepped out into the cement yard, which was the coolest part of the rest of the day to come, all of it belonging to her.

Sip was lying on the floor of the room he shared with his father in the next-door servants' quarters. Father was fast asleep on the bed, flat on his back with his mouth open in the round, whistling, toothless shape of all Sunday mornings since as far back as Sip could remember. There was the usual weekend odour of beer—beer excreted through the pores and carried on the breath and spilled carelessly over the front of his father's Saturday-night duds now crumpled in a heap at the foot of the bed. Sip took comfort in continuity, and even the morning-after soreness of his little body was, by now, more reassuring than not. In truth his father was a terror when drunk but luckily he only had the funds to achieve this exalted state of affairs once a week and Sip was resigned to his violent rages.

It was getting lighter and hotter in the airless room with its single window set so high in the cement wall that it mostly opened onto the eaves and a small bit of broken sky, high above and far away as ever.

Sip held his finger at arm's length. He closed one eye and then the other, watching his finger jump from side to side in the air before him, and when he'd tired of this sport he began to practise crossing his eyes using the bridge of his nose as an anchor. Time passed and he slowly grew hungry and then ferociously so. There was a tin of jam on the bedside table and sliced bread in a plastic bag from three days before, but Sip carefully cut away the mould and made himself two sandwiches so oozy with jam that he had to eat them hurriedly and leaning well forward between his knees. Afterwards he licked each finger then turned his attention to the floor. Some smears of jam had made their way onto the cement floor, it was true, but the floor itself was so encrusted with a week's worth of filth and so sticky with a weekend's worth of booze that they hardly signified.

Okay, thought Sip, and he went to fill a galvanized bucket from the outside tap. Miriam had given him a small bottle of washing-up liquid and he hoarded this amongst his treasures: his sewing notions and sketches, the beloved Annabel and a box of Chiclets that he'd had for going on six months now and that was still a quarter full, on account of how he bit each piece of gum in half and could make it last for almost ever. Now he squeezed four drops of the washing-up liquid into the bucket of water and began to lather the two together until he'd achieved a meagre froth of bubbles on the surface of the water. Nodding to himself gravely and careful not to disturb his father with the squeak of the galvanized bucket—

because though he slept like the dead for most and sometimes all of Sunday it was these unexpected household noises that jarred him, and he was a lion when roused—Sip dipped a rag into the soapy water and began to clear small earnest circles on the grimy cement floor.

Sometime later Sip set out, gleaming and clean as a dish. He had squeezed a drop of the washing-up liquid into his tooth mug and scrubbed his face until it shone. Yes, and all over his head too, digging into his scalp with his fingers and then cleaning his nails until his fingertips tingled, with an old corn scrubber Miriam had given him. Then he'd taken a pinch of his father's snuff and sneezed for a couple of minutes until even his nose felt as clean as a whistle. Father had expressly forbidden Sip from messing with his snuff under pain of a dreadful thrashing, the worst he'd ever had and maybe even much worse than that, but there was little chance of him noticing the minuscule amounts that disappeared every Sunday morning and even less of him carrying through with his threats when drunken bravado gave way to self-pity as it did by the time evening rolled around, you could count on it.

And besides, Sip was as incapable of withstanding temptation as the sun was of boiling up the dust that even now hung about the street in great hazy clouds of shimmering heat. It was still early in the morning but every now

Nightwatching

and then Sip would have to take out his handkerchief and wipe away the sweat from the back of his neck, and each time he did this he paused first to sniff at the handkerchief over which he had patted out a couple of drops of Old Spice Aftershave Lotion. The bottle had been sitting on the single shelf in the cement bathroom for as long as Sip could remember, right next to the tin of snuff over which so many threats and prohibitions and disobediences had intersected, and its opaque white glass and rather gummy grey stopper were as familiar to him as his own solemn face peering into the crazed glass above the cracked and leaking basin. His father had once been a dandy and those Friday nights when he'd stepped from the room they shared in a mist of Old Spice Aftershave Lotion still caused Sip to catch his breath in admiration, yoh weh!

He was looking for Ruthie because it hadn't escaped his attention that the bicycle beneath the privet hedge was missing and for a while he just walked along briskly, his hands in the pockets of his shorts, trying to keep to the shady part of the street. But she wasn't in the park—he hardly expected her to be, the park was always full of Sunday morning families and after-church folks, two kinds of people that Ruthie despised—and she wasn't on Bleeker Street or even hanging around the Greek Caffy, although by now it was midday and Mr. Papadopoulos had just pulled back the heavy

{179}

shutters and was unlocking the door and some ousies and even a couple of madams who'd forgotten to buy milk for the weekend were waiting outside. "Come in, come in, ladies," Mr. Papadopoulos was saying to the madams. Sip waited for the ousies to make their way, chattering and laughing, into the dim store, and then he slipped in behind them.

Although he'd only done it once before—the Chiclets—the mood was upon him and Sip felt powerful and capable of anything and at the same time small and invisible. You had to be both to achieve what he was planning to achieve and in addition bear a certain calm disregard for consequences, and for a long time now, Sip had felt himself to be buoyed only by the present moment. The past turned back on itself and the future jumped forward but both ran on and on without him. Even when the terrible old woman at the tok-tokkie house had been shaking him half to death, he'd only felt shock at the surprise of the ambush and not consternation or dread at what might follow. For who cared what happened to old Sip? No one anywhere and for as long as he could remember. So what?

Strange to say these desultory thoughts gave him courage and as a result he moved through the world with a sort of loose-shouldered self-reliance that surfaced now in this dim store as he sidled up behind the ousies who were clustered around the fridge and who were busily banging the heavy doors open and shut far more than was required to extract a pint or two of buttermilk or a couple of bottles of cream soda. Soon Mr. Papadopoulos would begin bellowing at them and they, in turn, would heckle the old Greek and all would be as it always was on a Sunday in the Greek Caffy around noon. Every time the fridge opened vapour billowed out, causing great merriment amongst the ousies, who knew that Mr. Papadopoulos must keep his temper in check until he'd finished serving the white madams: "Thank you, Mevrou Terheyden. Good day, good day."

Sip was crouching next to a rack of magazines. He was waiting for the white madams to leave, their car keys swinging importantly against plastic bags of last-minute milk and orange juice and floury dinner rolls. Then the old Greek would turn with his raised forefinger and his guttural anger and the ousies would pretend to cower behind hands that failed to stifle their guffaws. Sip was waiting for the perfect moment because he'd set his heart on the chocolate cigarettes that he'd seen some of the school kids "smoking" at morning break. They were all the rage; they were the pinnacle of his heart's desire and they were arranged in racks beneath the counter along with the bubble gum and the licorice, chocolate bars, nigger balls and packets of coloured sherbet.

After a while Sip grew tired of gazing at the candy and turned his attention to the wooden rack at the back of the store that was filled with magazines with different things on the covers: girls in bikinis, roast chicken dinners, more girls, more bikinis, cars with girls on top, tractors—no girls. There was a bunch of comics for kids and there, slap-bang in the middle, was a row of the photo romances that Ruthie liked.

Oh, thought Sip breathing out, and he made his mind a blank, still as a lake with no thoughts to skip like stones across its surface, then slipped the top magazine from the rack. But he was unlucky. The old Greek had hardly begun his wrangling with the ousies when he caught the movement from the corner of the store where Sip hunched behind the dusty shelves of Koo peaches and apricot jam and expensive bottles of Mrs. Ball's Chutney, or maybe it was the slight rusty squeak of the magazine rack that he heard beneath the hilarity of the women and their ribald tomfoolery, but he turned and made out the boy crouched like a runner at the starting gate and holding the rolled-up photo romance to his chest.

"Picannin!" yelled Mr. Papadopoulos, trying to lumber from behind his counter as Sip threw himself forward, because this was a race to the death, anyone could see that; the Caffy owner had turned red with rage, the colour of a rag to a bull although Sip was no bull, no kind of bull at all. And, "Run, picannin!" yelled the ousies in gleeful mockery. "Run, picannin, picannin, picannin!" as Sip gathered

Nightwatching

a final burst of speed and, with one hand outstretched to grab at the packets of sweeties in passing, swerved through the open door just as Mr. Papadopoulos fought free of his counter and lunged at the retreating figure, hurling epithets and hastily snatched potatoes with equal force.

Some four blocks on and Sip could no longer hear Mr. Papadopoulos. He stopped and leaned over, his hands on his knees, and panted sincerely until the world had stopped humming in his ears and he'd caught his breath, or what was left of it. The sun blazed up through the road until his feet burned through the thin soles of his takkies. *Run!* the road seemed to be saying, *Get going!* But Sip was tired, worn out, first from his vigilance in the store and then from that moment when Mr. Papadopoulos had turned around and fixed him with his terrible red-rimmed eyes, and then finally with the effort of the mad dash that had hurled him out of the store, away from Mr. Papadopoulos's reaching hands and down the street and here, here on this square of burning sidewalk.

But he was still clutching in one hand the photo romance and in the other the box of chocolate cigarettes he'd snatched from the counter. Well, okay. Sip straightened up and peered off into the distance to where a lonely traffic light blinked red and yellow and green although no cars were anywhere in sight. Then, the photo romance rolled up and poking from one pocket and the box of chocolate cigarettes bouncing from one hand to the other—*tskah*, *tskah*—he set off down the street at a steady clip. Presently he remembered what the old Greek had called him, that familiar word, and his feet found a bright new rhythm on the pavement. *Picannin, picannin, picannin, oh, picannin.*

Temperance Thandile was already an hour late but she hadn't sent word to cancel her visit and Miriam was still hopeful. Already Miriam had walked to the gate and back three times and once to the corner of Unicor Road, from where, if she visored her eyes with one hand, she could see all the way to the highway from which direction she expected her daughter to arrive. There was no bus stop on Ontdekkers so the people were used to walking along the side of the highway on their way into town from the Location. The men walked swiftly and the women only as swiftly as they were able because they often carried children on their backs and bundles on their heads. Ah, but not Temperance Thandile, thought Miriam, the second time she found herself hastening to the corner of the street, not Temperance Thandile who was young and unimpeded by babies and bundles and the way they pressed down on a life, turning the road beneath one's feet into the long black distance between yesterday and forever.

Nightwatching

"Mama! Hey, Mama, have you lost something?" Her daughter was leaning against a rusty Chevrolet that had drawn up to the house from the other end of the service road and, true to the youthful perversity of her nature, was holding her sides with laughter.

Tcha, thought Miriam, an hour late and a world of rudeness. And who was this emerging from the driver's seat so that he too could wave at Miriam, though with some deference, at least, as befitted an older woman and the mother of the girl he'd driven all the way to see this mother, for a reason she could not yet discern. Courtship? Kindness? Seduction? Or merely as a favour to her brother Jonas—for now that her eyes were growing accustomed to the late-afternoon sunlight she could make out the boy, Clanwilliam, who worked in Mr. Blackburn's Concession Store and who was, once again, tentatively lifting his hand to greet Miriam.

"Where you off to, Mama?" called her daughter. "Don't you remember that I'm supposed to visit this afternoon?" And once again she rocked on her heels with mirth, turning to Clanwilliam as if to say, *Ho, fella, is it not good to be young rather than old and without humour?* Her daughter was wearing a bright sundress with a halter round the neck, yellow, with cherries and strawberries and slices of watermelon, and on her feet wedged orange sandals. Was it her

{185}

daughter's ambition to resemble a bowl of fruit, thought Miriam, juicy and abundant and ripe for the plucking?

She nodded at Clanwilliam. "How are your people?" she asked, not only out of politeness but also to remind him that in the matter of her daughter he did not act alone but as one who was a person because of other people. These were the words of the old African proverb that had meant so much to Thandile's late father and that Albert Tsomela had repeated to his children until the words rattled one against the other. Stones to pocket and hold on to. *A person is a person because of other people.*

"They are well, ma." Clanwilliam snatched off his cloth cap and looked ashamed of his part in her daughter's merriment. At least Miriam *thought* he looked ashamed, but it was difficult to tell with the sun in her eyes and now, what was this? This new development altogether? Her daughter was leaning into the car where Miriam could suddenly see that there was another passenger lounging in the front seat and, quick as a kiss, she took her leave of him. Yes, it was a man, of that you could be certain, a man slouched low down so as to frustrate recognition.

Miriam shaded her brow with one hand and peered into the front seat of the Chevrolet where the man was holding a brown-paper-wrapped bottle in front of his face. Sipping, yes, but concealing himself too so that it was all Miriam could do not to reach into the car and simply snatch the bottle from his hands. Then she thought of her young daughter, her Temperance Thandile, driving down the highway wedged between these two men, one known and the other too (for why else was he skulking between the dash and the brow of his cap yanked down low to meet each long pull from the brown paper bag?). Known, yes, but hidden until she could draw concealment aside like a curtain.

"Awah, it is you, is it, Harry Ditsebe," said Miriam growing impatient with her thoughts and finally reaching into the car and pushing the bottle away from his mouth. "And how is my good friend, Sophie Ditsebe?" For was this man who dawdled in the front seat of the Chevrolet sucking liquor from the bottle as if he were a baby, was he not the husband of poor Sophie, whose longing for a child had turned her sour as last week's milk? But Harry Ditsebe just slouched lower in his seat and made no reply and presently Miriam turned on her heel and hastened after Temperance Thandile, that bright girl whose yellow sundress with the sun shining through from behind had turned into a glowing net that caught her swaying haunches and firm buttocks in its golden transparency.

"Humba khale, ma," muttered Clanwilliam. "Go well."

By the time Miriam caught up with her daughter, Thandile was sitting forward on her mother's bed and examining the meal that her mother had prepared, taking into account all of her favourite treats such as white bread sandwiches, some with sardines, some with apricot jam, a bowl of Hanepoot grapes, and a tin of Eagle Brand condensed milk. There was a kettle ready to boil on the hot plate in case she preferred tea as Miriam did, but also a couple of bottles of Mr. Blackburn's Coca-Cola in case, as was more likely, she did not. The food was carefully spread out on an empty crate that Miriam had transformed with a hand-stitched tablecloth and napkins, and the dishes and cups all matched because they had been borrowed from the Blackburn kitchen cupboards where they would be returned later that evening, washed and dried and good as new.

Temperance Thandile was staring dreamily into space. She had kicked off one orange wedged sandal and was rubbing her instep to ease the pain brought on by maintaining her balance and walking and keeping her shoes on all at the same time, which none but the young experience—though what else is youth for, thought Miriam indulgently, and for how long does it last?

"Have a sardine sandwich, my daughter," she offered now, "or are you ready for your condensed milk?"

"Mama," groaned Temperance, and she suddenly grabbed her mouth with both hands and limped as quickly as she could, but with the lopsided gait of a girl who still

Nightwatching

has one shoe on and one shoe off, to the little cement bathroom where she hung over the toilet bowl discharging her stomach in rattling volleys.

"Hau, Mama!" Pale and shaky, Thandile hobbled back into the room and hoisted herself onto her mother's bed. One sandal was still strapped to her foot and in the small dark room with its single bottle-glass window, too high and too thick to let in much of anything let alone light, the orange wedged sandals—one on her foot, the other tumbled sideways on the floor—seemed to glow and pulse slightly.

Miriam looked at her daughter, looked hard. "And how far along are you, Temperance Thandile?" she asked.

"Tcha, Mama, what nonsense is this? Can't a girl get sick if she feels like it, can't a girl fall ill?"

And she poured herself a glass of Coca-Cola, but Miriam noticed that she added two heaped spoonfuls of sugar, then stirred vigorously to flatten out the bubbles. Two months, she thought to herself, two and a half at most. She was still so young, this daughter of hers, only seventeen, and instead of the unnatural heat of her body, and at other times the cool dryness, her forehead felt sweaty and her hands clammy.

"Tcha, Mama," she snapped and snatched her hands away.

"Oh, Thandile, Thandi . . . ," mourned Miriam softly,

but then she suddenly remembered all the Milo-eyed, fuzzy-haired babies she'd brought into the world, their curly mouths and warm, humming tummies.

Well, she thought, seventeen is not old but it's not so young, not so very young.

The last time she'd looked into her daughter's eyes (and even the time before that), the double suns had been shining steadily. Not burning up, not burning out. Well, okay. So, a baby.

Despite herself Miriam's heart lifted and she lost herself for a time in pleasurable anticipation. The sour-milk smell, the delicious flesh of infant thighs and infant wrists, and, oh, the toes, all the little wriggling, pop-in-the-mouth toes! Thandile had curled up sideways on the bed and fallen asleep, looked like, her hand beneath her cheek. Miriam eased the heavy sandal off her daughter's foot and drew a blanket up over her. How strange that she should be restored to her mother at this moment, as peaceful and serene as a sleeping child. And, after all, Miriam herself hadn't been much older—only two years—when she'd become a mother for the first time; which is what she must tell Jericho, yes, and Jonas too, for the one brother would be angry and the other hurt, according to their natures.

Who is he, she could already imagine Jericho exclaiming bitterly, *this man whose carelessness has ended my sister's career?*

Well, if not her career then at least her youth! Jonas might retort because he knew better than Jericho of Thandile's ambition to remain a shopgirl perhaps forever or at least until she had discovered what ever was for.

But Clanwilliam was a good man, she must explain to her sons, a person who was a person—in the words of their father—for other people. Well, she certainly hoped so. Miriam took a small bite of an apricot jam sandwich because she didn't care for the sweetness or the stickiness of the white bread sandwich but she was suddenly ravenous. She pictured Clanwilliam leaning against the car with the light of the afternoon sun behind him. She'd shamed him into pulling off his cloth cap and wishing her well. If a man was capable of being shamed then what might a woman not accomplish on his behalf? It was the shameless ones who couldn't be reached, either by kindness or by anger, and here Miriam thought of that foolish tsotsi, that Harry Ditsebe slouched between the lip of his bottle and the rim of his cap. No wonder poor Sophie Ditsebe had acquired a bitter disposition and a reputation for mean-spirited dealings amongst the Saturday-afternoon women, for how long had she suffered that shameless fool—first his bad-tempered lounging-about presence in her life and then his month-long absences without so much as a by-your-leave or a *so long, baba* or a pay packet to see her through. And no baby either, which was the true cause, Miriam had always believed, of poor Sophie Ditsebe's eternal disgruntlement.

Ayah, Miriam sighed now, slowly licking the apricot jam from her fingers. It wasn't easy being a woman, but then the good Lord hadn't asked her opinion in this matter. He hadn't given her a choice, although if he *had*—*if* he had—here Miriam was obliged to crinkle up her forehead in perplexity, for if she deplored the conditions of her existence and the meagre circumstances of her influence, yet she was still unable to imagine a better life.

She thought of all the people she knew: the miners who faced darkness and death underground, and the domestic workers, the maids and gardeners and kitchen boys, who laboured all day in the houses of white people and who slept at night in the servants' quarters of these same houses, in cement rooms that were too small for anything except half-forgotten dreams and cockroaches and the prairie moon on its way past a single cracked window set much too high up in the wall. Rooms too small for the children and the hope for their future, which was boundless. And too small for love that huddled in a heap on the floor or stared through the eyes of children too young to have seen so much. Quite so much. She thought of Sip, and even of Ruthie, and then she thought of all the Saturday-afternoon babies who kicked and smiled in the crooks of

Nightwatching

their mothers' arms for a time, for a short summer season, and then were gone. And Jericho, whose heart was breaking for his people and whose solution was the struggle. And Jonas, whose heart was breaking too but who only said "work harder." Jericho and Jonas, both heartbroken, and now this sister of theirs, this Temperance Thandile, two months heavy, maybe two and a half.

She must have been staring with great concentration at her sleeping daughter because Thandile opened her eyes, bridging the gap between sleeping and waking suddenly, as she had always done.

"What, Mama?" she asked in reply to the question that she saw hovering on her mother's lips.

"This Clanwilliam, now," Miriam began, "he has a good job in Mr. Blackburn's store and he comes from honest people. Yes, and I believe he is a kind man. I *believe* so but that is for you to tell me."

"Yes, Mama," said Thandile in a muffled voice. "Clanwilliam is very kind."

Her shoulders were shaking, which surprised Miriam for when had her daughter ever trembled with shame or with fear? But then she remembered how she had felt when she was carrying her children, sometimes as vast and proud as the sun around which all the planets revolved, sometimes as small and cold and lost as a stone.

Oh, the poor child, thought Miriam and she took her daughter in her arms. Years had passed between the little girl whose stubborn head had fitted under her mother's chin and the "grown-up already" half-girl half-woman she'd become, and in between there'd been a few hugs but mostly Thandile's cranky, pulling-away nature had held her mother at a distance, so this embrace was like the return of a lover. Miriam bent her head and inhaled the smell of her daughter's scalp and pressed her cheek to the firm-fleshed apple of Thandile's cheek and tried to soothe the trembling, but to no avail. On the contrary, the more she patted her back, the more Thandile seemed to shake until, finally, her mother pulled away so that she could look into her daughter's eyes the better to calm her. But what she saw there made her draw in her breath sharply— awah! The girl wasn't shaking with fear but with laughter. Not shame but glee.

"This Clanwilliam is truly kind, Mama," Thandile continued, as if there had been no interruption. "He looks after me at the store and he shows me how to make change for the customers. He tells me where to put my coat and handbag and where to eat my lunch. He tells me, 'Don't wear high heels, Sisi, you'll only get sore feet,' and at other times he looks at me like this, like *this*"—Thandile made a comical face—"and he says, 'Don't wear such a short skirt, Sisi, do you want the mine boys to look at your legs all day long?'"

Her laughter was as carefree and unrestrained as it had once been, before the little boy and the tree and the windmilling arms and the leg broken in two places and the girl she'd fought for the boy she hadn't wanted anyway and the double suns burning their way to extinction in her eyes.

"But do you know why he's the kindest man in all the world, Mama? Mama? Because only today he stopped to give us a lift when he saw us walking along the highway."

And now she was laughing frankly. Frankly, and with no attempt at disguise.

"What is that you say, Mama? Mama? Are you asking who was accompanying me down the highway when Clanwilliam, this kindest Clanwilliam of all, stopped to offer a lift into town? Why it was Harry Ditsebe, of course. My friend Harry Ditsebe was walking with me. We often walk together, Mama, me and Harry Ditsebe. We are the best of friends, the very best."

By the time Sip got to the water reservoir the afternoon was well along and he was so hot and thirsty from the long walk that even just the smell of damp rising out of the vast storage tank was a relief. Ruthie was under her usual tree, knees drawn up against her chest, chin on her knees, and when she saw him she scowled him one of her fiercest scowls, whose familiarity, too, was a sort of relief.

"Oh, go away!" she yelled when he tried to sit down next to her. "Just scram, kid."

She meant business, no question. Ruthie was always irritable with Sip but sometimes her irritation was habitual, a dog barking at the new moon, and could be cajoled away or waited out, and sometimes it was particular and required a particular sort of humility, but today it was just plain vicious. She picked up a stone, biggest she could find, and threw it at him.

When Ruthie began with her stone-throwing, Sip always made himself scarce, quickest way possible and dignity to the winds. Because after the stones came the fists. It had happened; he'd been there. But today he was just too damn tired. Too damn tired to run and too damn tired to scramble up and hobble away in the roaring heat and even too tired, if it came to that, to duck when the stone came flying and hit him on the side of his head just beneath his eye.

Sip never cried; it was one of the strictest rules he lived by and he'd kept to that resolution for years and he kept to it still. Oh, but he was tired, though, and small, and what a boy less fierce than he might call mournful.

Nightwatching

"Picannin," he whispered to cheer himself up. "Hey, how about a smoke, picanniny?"

He sat down in the farthest bit of shade from Ruthie and extracted a chocolate cigarette from his box. The bluegum tree above their heads threw down quick spatters of light and shade until the whole world seemed to skittle and swirl. In the long grass the crickets sawed and sawed at the ragged edges of the afternoon. Sip lay on his back and listened to the peculiar engine thrum of heat that was like the sound of electricity surging through the pylons that marched across the veld with their terrible skull-and-crossbones and their warning signs—DANGER! GEVAAR! INGOZI! Today these same warnings were scattered everywhere he looked around the perimeter of the water reservoir. Visitors were STRICTLY PROHIBITED, as the signs clearly indicated, and as for the trespassers, why, they would be PROSECUTED TO THE FULL EXTENT OF THE LAW.

Ruthie lay on her stomach and began to torment an ant that had wandered through the roots of the kikuyu grass. She put out a finger and stopped it in its tracks. The ant changed direction again and again, its delicate antennae prodding her alien fingertips. Suddenly it seemed to make up its mind and with the blind instinct of its kind clambered onto the surface of her hand. Dispassionately Ruthie watched the ant make its way laboriously towards the centre of her palm and begin to follow the mysterious rut of her lifeline.

"You know I could die if it gets to the end of this here line," she informed Sip, who still watched her every move with a dreamy half-smile on his soft child's face. "Die, just like that. And why?" She beckoned him over and then, when he was crouching at her side, she thrust her palm with its wobbling black ant close to his face. "I bet you don't even know what these lines mean, hey."

Sip peered at her hand dimly then opened his own.

"Here, let me look. Oh my goodness! Oh my good golly gosh! Oh, Sip, my poor little fellow!" Ruthie pushed Sip's hand away as if what she had scried in his palm was too terrible to behold.

"Awah, Ruthie, you don't frighten me." But his voice trembled a little and his eyes widened as he watched the ant trundle again to the middle of her lifeline, where, yet again, she halted its progress with an imperious forefinger and lifted it back to its starting point.

"No, look, now see here. Do you want me to tell you what these lines mean? This is my heart line and this is my head line. See how they're joined in the middle? That's the sign of good luck. All the most famous people in the history of the world have had a heart line and a head line joined up just like mine. Madame Curie and Mother Teresa and that Elizabeth Taylor you like so much . . . everyone you can think of. Now I'm not saying it's a guarantee of famousness, I'm not saying that. But one thing I *will* say is that I've never heard of anyone famous who hasn't had this heart line and head line joining up thing. Well?"

Sip had been peering, for some time, into the enigma of his palm with a worried half-smile still ghosting his lips. Suddenly he made up his mind and with a swift air of resolve presented his right hand as if he were giving over a parcel, and one, moreover, of which he was anxious to rid himself. Ruthie gazed at it for some moments, puffing her cheeks out and blowing at her fringe. She yanked his hand this way and that, first pulling it up close to her nose and then angling it out towards the light, then up to her nose again for she was, first and foremost, a showman and she liked to set the stage for her malarkey.

"Hmm, as to the head line and heart line crossing, I will say I'm surprised by that. That I will say." She *was* too. What could old Sip find to be famous for? Scrawniness, runtiness? Sewing, maybe? Well, well. She looked down at her own palm and tried to remember what she'd once read in the film magazines she regularly checked out at the Greek Caffy whenever old Papadopoulos fell into his afternoon slump behind the counter. *Do You Have Famous Hands? The Secrets of Chiromancy. What Do the Palms Foretell?* Something like that. The stupid ant was still wobbling along the rut of her lifeline. Ruthie eased it carefully onto the ground and then gently, precisely, benevolently, squashed it flat.

"No, but what worries me is this. See here how short your lifeline is? And how it ends off suddenly—well, it's difficult to tell with black people but it certainly looks sudden to me. Certainly does. Now I don't want to worry you, I wouldn't want to worry you, and anyway there's nothing you can do about it, is there?"

"I'm not worried," said Sip.

"Good, because there's nothing you can do about it anyhow. It's called fate and fate is what's written in the stars and the, the planets and the palms of folks' hands, which in *your* case, I'm sorry to tell you, is not good news, but like I said I wouldn't want to worry you."

"I'm not worried," repeated Sip. And it was true, he was not. The news of his impending fame cast out all other considerations and he moved and breathed now in a soft effulgence of hopefulness. "So head and heart cross," he breathed out, rocking himself slowly from side to side, "like Miss Elizabeth Taylor."

Ruthie was enraged. "But don't you care that you're going to die young? There, man, right in the middle of your life, it looks like. I'm trying to tell you but you're not listening. Death—there, *there*, THERE—right in the palm of your hand." In her rage Ruthie was stabbing at his hand with her forefinger. Her cheeks were red and she felt close to tears with frustration.

"And what do you think, you stupid boy? Do you think death's just like closing your eyes one night and not waking up in the morning? Let me tell you something I didn't want to tell you earlier, on account of not wanting to scare you, you silly little boy. Death *hurts*. There's blood and bodies torn open and noise and, and *worms* afterwards. And then when the worms have eaten you, the, the nothing begins. Just nothing and nothing and nothing for as long as it takes and then more nothing. Man, you have no idea! Do you think you'll be able to cut your patterns when you're dead? Do you think dead people sew and ride bikes and shoot marbles? An hour is a year when you're dead and a second is about a, a *million* years. And in the middle of all that nothing, all that terrible terrible nothing, if you could feel for just one moment do you know what you'd feel, Sip? Do you know? You'd probably want to come back to an afternoon just like this one."

She was gulping back her sobs as she spoke but the tears came anyway and the more unsuccessful she was at concealing them, the angrier she grew. "Just like this one," she began to yell now, pounding her fist into the palm of her hand. "This long, flat, bloody, boring afternoon with nothing to do from one end to another, but let me tell you it would be like heaven if you were in the middle of that terrible nothing I was telling you about. Why, you'd *beg* to come back to this park and lie on your back in the grass and look up at the sky."

Ruthie had no idea where her passion had sprung from. She seldom did these days. Oh, what was the matter with her bloody bloody self? One minute she was content to play lazy games and tease Sip about his lifeline and the next she had turned with the wind and then she couldn't stop until she'd blown herself out and even then. And all this business about death and worms and the everlasting nothingness?

Suddenly Ruthie yanked herself upright. "Come on," she tossed over her shoulder and started off for the stepladder that hung down over one side of the reservoir tank. Oh no, thought Sip. But he dusted himself off and followed her. He always did.

The stepladder didn't reach the ground but folded back and locked into place above their heads, and this was to stop *kids like them* from fooling around on the edge of the tank, fooling around and falling in and next thing drowning, which quite a lot of them had done over the years. Quite a lot but mostly at night, Sip comforted himself, for he couldn't swim and hated the dark, eager waters of the reservoir that seemed to draw him down down down whenever he balanced on the slimy lip of the concrete barrier.

Ruthie was still straining for the bottom rung of the stepladder, yelling all this time, yelling her head off: "Bloody!" and "Are you deaf, man, as well as blind?" and then a lot of things about the Lord that she'd never have dared to say in front of Miriam, no way. But Sip was pleased to see, which he could straight away, that the stepladder was locked up tight and too far above their heads to reach and this was because of the number of kids that had drowned—*yearly*, the newspapers said—ever since the town began keeping tally.

And what is this *yearly*? Miriam had exclaimed, slapping at the paper with one hand as it lay spread out before her on the kitchen table. She was cutting down a pumpkin to boil for supper, following the thick rind with her sharp kitchen knife, and each time she thought of this word, this *yearly*, she clucked again and tossed her head. Sip didn't know why.

Ruthie was in a terrible mood, even worse than when he first got there and that was saying a considerable amount. Yup, thought Sip, yebo. And he scrabbled back, silently, and settled down on his bottom some distance away to wait it out, because what else could he do? He loved her, that was all there was to it. He loved her but he didn't want to be hurt by her; he didn't want to be slapped or kicked or scratched by her and he didn't want the stones that she was flinging with great force at the water tank to ricochet off the rusty metal and hit him.

"Hey!" Ruthie turned around. "Come here. I've got an idea." She'd dragged an old oil drum to the stepladder and was trying to reach the lowest rung. It was out of her reach and not even just, but by quite a lot, which made her even more angry. At such times Sip thought he could hear the air around her head crackle and there was a faint smell like burnt toast.

"Come here," Ruthie called again, over her shoulder because she was busy fiddling with the oil drum so as to balance it more firmly on the ground. When he reached her, she got him to kneel down on the oil drum with his hands clasped together in the shape of her foot in preparation for a buckie-up. The plan was for Sip to lunge up, taking her with him, her hands on his shoulders then reaching, at the last moment, for the bottom rung of the stepladder. One smart push was all it would take, she assured him. "Come on, man," she urged, "stop fooling around."

But it didn't work. How could it? Sip was too small and too weak and though he panted and pushed and wrestled with the weight of Ruthie and did *not* unclasp his hands when she kicked him cruelly, he could not stagger to his feet. He could not stagger to his feet nor thrust the girl up by the soles of her feet and the strength of his arms nor send her soaring through the air above his head to fasten like a spider to one of the struts that held the water tank aloft. Instead, both of them fell over, fell hard, on either side of the oil drum, hitting the ground with an *oof-oof* like the sound of ambition gasping for air.

"Okay," said Ruthie, wiping the blood off her hands. "This time you've got to do it standing up."

The fourth time the thin, nervous bones of his body jolted hard into the earth, Sip allowed himself a small groan of pain, but Ruthie was pitiless. On him, on herself. She'd fallen as often as he and from as great a height and hit the ground as hard and lost her breath as much. Her shorts were stained with the blood she'd casually wiped away and her hair had come loose from its ponytail and was tousled first one way and then another across her sweaty forehead. Sip lay on his back and tried to breathe. The sky was far away, farther than it had ever been before. No longer a cool blue but white hot and pulsing with heat, and behind him the veld too jumped up and down between the legs of all the twitchy, thrumming insects that were or ever had been, their chirps and crackles and pops going on and on through the long afternoon.

"Come on," said Ruthie, "I've got an idea." And she hauled him up onto the oil drum again. Her idea was that he must just stand still and let her clamber onto his back.

Then there was to be more pushing—he had to push her *up* and *over* his head, but she didn't mention how—and then, and then . . .

By now, Ruthie had pulled herself onto his back. He could feel the saddle of her hard, narrow haunches about his waist and, for a moment, the heat of her breath against his cheek. Then she was kicking at his back and straining against a vertical strut. She lodged a knee in his shoulder, and her foot in its canvas tennis shoe jabbed hard at his ear as it flew past him.

For the fifth time that afternoon all the bones in Sip's body hit the ground at the same time, and jumped, each one in its separate socket, as if an electrical current had been earthed. For the fifth time Sip lay flat on his back and looked up at the sky.

"Told you," sang Ruthie, high above him. "*Told you* I could do it."

She was holding onto the stepladder with one hand and waving at him, but then she climbed a little higher and began fumbling at the twine that held the last rungs of the stepladder above the ground. It took a while, working on the twine with one hand—but what was time to Ruthie, who'd prevailed over the battered oil drum and the slippery water tank, and even old Sip, who was still lying on the ground like a shongololo worm, bewildered and exposed?

Nightwatching

"Hey, better get out of the sun, my little man," Ruthie called down in sudden good humour. She had the idea to link her arm around the rungs of the ladder, which would give her ballast while she worked on the twine with both hands. With a grating crash, the fastenings gave way and the last segment of the stepladder swung down. The clangour of metal against metal silenced thought, but when the last reverberations died down and the crickets began to snap and pop in the bushes again and the sun stopped tumbling in that forever spinning, blank and charmless sky, Sip got up slowly. He shaded his eyes with his hand but she was already halfway up the water tank, that old Ruthie, and climbing steadily upwards.

"No but where? Honestly, Miriam, has no one seen the child at all today?"

Lionel Blackburn had just poked his head around the side of the servant's quarters, which was something he hardly ever did, as Bettina Foley very well knew. From her bedroom where she lay tossing fitfully in the afternoon heat, with its window opened to catch any stray breeze that might be passing, she could hear his voice and discern the irritation if not the anxiety he must be feeling. Breeze or no breeze—and the latter was by far the more likely eventuality because Sundays, as she'd often had cause to observe, were strangely windless days: dense and close and becalmed upon the shoal of the week to come—Bettina was grateful today for the open window.

The sound of Lionel Blackburn's voice raised in incredulity gave her something to speculate upon and something—more to the point—to offer when she next saw her friend Annemarie Willems. *Ag, he's a good man,* she imagined herself telling Annemarie. *A good man, for what he is. But comes a girl, my friend, even that little tramp from Bloem, and you watch what happens next. Now he's gone and misplaced the kid. No one's seen her all day and if that Ruthven doesn't bear watching then I don't know who does, tcha. Poor motherless child, no one to give a sweet how d'you do excepting that hoity-toity Miriam, no-account ousie that she is.*

But the effort to bear arms on Ruthie's behalf was doomed to failure. In truth the music teacher could not stomach the child: the dash of her hand against the front door knocker, the sharp rumble as she drew the piano stool towards her each week, the occasional—yet far too frequent—bang of the piano lid against the end of endeavour. She was all angular bones and bouncing knees and twitches and jerks and noise, noise, noise. Why, the sounds she pulled out of that poor upright, that dear familiar, were an abomination. Yes, an abomination, thought Bettina, pleased with herself. Like one of the monstrous creatures described in Leviticus. An animal that did not chew the cud but that walked about on cleft hooves, ha!

It was hot in this late part of the afternoon but Bettina had no cause for complaint. Every Sunday afternoon, after she played piano accompaniment to the hymns in the Methodist church near Weltevreden Primary School, she would return home and take a light meal—just a small luncheon salad, tomatoes and cukes, a little sour cream—*You know me*, she'd inform anyone who asked, though few enough did, and even fewer upon hearing this interesting arrangement would urge, *Oh, but come home with us and have a real Sunday pot roast, do*. Few enough, but once or twice it had happened and so she lived in hope. But today, once again, nobody had asked and she'd returned to her cluttered little house and opened the windows to let out all the heat and some of the emptiness and then she'd sat on the edge of her bed and removed her Warner's deluxe gusseted "two-way."

It was a formidable foundation garment and it compressed her flesh into the stately tube of which she approved, pushing up her bosom and flattening out her stomach and squeezing her buttocks together until she appeared to be a sort of moulded plastic idea of femininity. Bettina liked the way the deluxe gusseted two-way armoured her against the world, fragile woman that she was, and she appreciated the manner in which it disguised her flaws—*Face it, we all have them, Annemarie, my dear*—and heightened her assets. But, ah, what she most relished about her two-way was the feeling of ease she achieved when, with a hand clasped against her spine and made deft through habit, she unhooked an intricate line of hooks and eyes and the garment opened in two shell-like halves.

On warm Sunday afternoons she would allow herself this luxury of unfettered flesh, lying on her narrow bed, half dreaming, in dressing gown and slippers with the two-way still warm from her body hung in its hinged halves over a chair. How her stomach would gurgle and unpleat, how softly her suddenly free breasts would fall against her chest, first in one position and then another, for she often turned restlessly, stirred by the heat and the strange windless, birdless silence of the Lord's Day and the odd feel of the thin nylon fabric of her dressing gown against her bare skin. At these times it was not unusual for the nylon to irritate her breasts until the nipples swelled and then hardened uncomfortably. Oh, those large brown nipples of hers. Teats! How they shamed her.

A burst of laughter sounded from the house next door. Two different kinds of laughter: first a woman's, silly and spoon-like. Spoon-like? Well now, thought Bettina, surprising herself. But the woman's laughter sounded just like a cheap spoon knocking against the side of a tin mug. As for the man's laugh that accompanied Miss Silly Spoons (ha, that was good, she must remember to tell Annemarie!), of one thing she was certain: the head that threw itself back and the mouth that opened wide to release this merriment upon the world (as if the world didn't have troubles enough, she thought spitefully)—in short, the head and the mouth and the laughter—none of these belonged to Lionel Blackburn. He was not naturally mirthful, thought Bettina, and that was the regrettable fact of the matter.

Must be the brother, then, the laughing brother. She'd caught glimpses of him all through the weekend, the merest glimmers of his comings and goings with Lionel Blackburn and the curly-headed tramp in tow. But on Saturday night she'd actually heard him talking to the terrible Blackburn girl. And then the two of them had climbed into the pretty red sports car and whirled off down the dirt road to the highway. Could this really have happened?

"Oh that Ruthven is a law unto herself," she often complained to Annemarie, "a trial and a tribulation without end."

"Ag, juffie," Annemarie would chide at these times, "what have you got against the poor girl besides the fact that she hates to practise her piano pieces?"

"But, but, surely that's the point, man," Bettina would stutter to cover her confusion. "She wants to play piano, she must practise. Every month I have to say to her father, 'Lionel,' I say, 'I am trying my best with your daughter but she is not trying with me.' Oh yes"—she turned once again to Annemarie—"she does not *try* but she is certainly *trying*."

Annemarie laughed and gave her friend a sly pinch on the forearm. "But perhaps your Mr. Blackburn does not care so much for the music as he does for the music teacher!"

Although she was a good friend and an often congenial companion, Annemarie had a silly high-pitched laugh that frequently grated on Bettina's finely tuned ears. And, in addition, although she hardly liked to admit it even to herself, Bettina had come to suspect that Annemarie had taken a lover recently and the thought filled her with revulsion. She had no doubt that he was ugly or married or both, or why would her friend hide him, but in any case her disgust was at once less rational and more powerful than mere fastidiousness could explain. It was of the sort that made one's gorge rise as at the sight of skin forming on the surface of a cup of hot milk, and Bettina could not, during this last galling exchange, suppress a ladylike shudder, which she took pains not to conceal from her friend. Go ahead, let her ask!

But Mr. Blackburn, now. In truth, Bettina admired Lionel Blackburn's taciturnity, his mournfulness, his general air of stern if kindly solitariness for which she was inclined to blame his daughter. Well, if it was not precisely the girl's fault then it was certainly to her advantage that her poor father had never remarried, never courted, never so much as looked at another woman after his dear wife died. Until now, of course, and it beggared description to think what all those abstemious years had brought him. The tramp, thought Bettina newly outraged, the stinking bloody bitch!

It was only in the privacy of her bedroom that she allowed her uncensored thoughts to waft upwards like the breezes she longed for, to stir the dull heaviness of Sunday afternoons. And the freedom of her loose-fleshed body turning over and over in the thin nylon dressing gown honed her hatred into a hard poking thing. "Oh, tramp," she groaned, squeezing her breasts hard. "Bloody, bloody bitch!"

Ruthie sat on the concrete lip of the water tank and dangled her legs. The lip was just wide enough for a kid to perch upon and hunch forward as Ruthie was now doing. She didn't really want to touch the dark, greasy-looking water with its sudden iridescent gleams but she wanted to frighten Sip who was sitting with his legs drawn up and his eyes widening with every downward feint she made.

"Hey, what's that?" she called suddenly, making him jump. "There, over *there*, man. Something green and, and rotten. Oh-oh, looks like another bloater. Ho-boy, that's gonna be some stink! Get ready to upchuck, my little man, because that looks like it's gonna be the stinkiest kid yet."

Sip was torn. He didn't like to spoil her fun but after the first sincere shock that was like the earth jolting through his bones again, he just plain did not believe her. Did not. But she was his Ruthie, his love, and so he tried to oblige, opening his eyes wide until they were all floating irises and his mouth was as round as a giant zero to indicate that nothing, *nothing* like this had ever happened before.

"Oh, quit it," said Ruthie crossly. "Just stop your fooling around now."

So that hadn't worked out and Sip was chagrined until he remembered the box of chocolate cigarettes he'd pushed deep into his pocket. "Want a smoke?" he asked casually, taking only a moment to admire the crisp cellophane wrapping and the deeply satisfying rustle of the chocolate cigarettes rubbing together—*tskah, tskah, tskah.*

Ruthie made him throw her the packet and she caught it with one hand. "Hoo-wee," she called out, "good thing it didn't fall into the water, hey."

Sip looked down into the water. The walls of the great water tank went straight down and even at the concrete lip were slimy to the touch, although much slimier farther down and with a neon blaze of moss at the water's edge. There was no wind but the water seemed to be moving, although in no particular direction that he could tell and for no particular reason. But moving. Like an animal with smooth muscles moving easily beneath its black skin. If he fell into the water tank the animal would swallow him down in two gulps and that would be the end of Sip until his body filled up with poisonous gases and he rose to the surface, bright green and rolling and inflamed, like a single eye stuck in the animal's forehead.

Ruthie flipped open the cigarette box and extracted a chocolate cigarette, tapping it against her nail the way she'd seen a film star do. The cigarette sounded just fine so she delicately inserted it between the middle and index fingers of her right hand. She'd done this many times before, smoking chewed-down pencils and school pens, dreaming in the back row of her Standard Four class, Mrs. Bakkes yelling, "Ruthven, *Ruth*ven, are we *tres*passing upon your time again, you *stu*pid girl!" Sometimes she even smoked drinking straws, making wide gestures and clutching her hand to her *bosoms* and saying, *My dear, but how* fas*cinating!* But mostly what she liked were the half-smoked cigarettes that the commercial travellers left behind after their poker games. There were always two or three of these, scattered about the living room ashtrays in various states of stubbed-out usefulness, and she'd learned to resuscitate them by carefully straightening them out and setting them quickly aflame with a kitchen match from the box that Miriam kept under the sink.

In the dark of her bedroom she'd sit forward tensely on the edge of her bed and draw at her butts, sending the smoke in thin streams towards the open window and into the night. It had taken her a while to acquire a taste for the dratted things; it wasn't easy, but she persevered. Ruthie was like that—tenacious. Didn't matter how many times she fell off that stupid oil drum either or how much her leg ached after the fourth time she fell (and that time awkwardly). Pain was the thing you held onto when you'd given everything else away. Besides, in Ruthie's limited experience pain was the one thing you could call your own since no one else was in such a tearing hurry to take it away from you.

But it had taken quite a long time to learn to enjoy the cigarettes. Much longer than other tastes, like olives and pickled cucumbers and tinned asparagus, and certainly much longer than brandy and Coca-Cola, which had, in fact, taken Ruthie less than no time at all to acquire a wholly unfeigned distaste for. Well, but cigarettes, now there was elegance! Elegance and wealth and the glittering Life to Come. And besides, cigarettes stopped you from growing; it was a proven fact as Miriam took huffy pains to point out— you couldn't put one over on old Miri—which was precisely the reason that Ruthie kept picking diligently through the ashtrays and dirty saucers for smoked-down butts after the commercial travellers had left and her father had retired to his room, yawning, "Well, time to turn in now, my girl, and shouldn't you . . . ?" Growing was the bane of her existence at present—too tall, too fast, too poky out in front—and Ruthie was good at grand plans, yes, but she'd also learned the value of short-term solutions.

By now the candy cigarette was gnawed down to nothing at all and the gully between her index and middle finger was slick with chocolate. Feeling generous, she hurled the cigarette box back at Sip—*tskah, tskah, tskah*. The boy, who'd been watching her intently and surreptitiously imitating her gestures—even going so far as to tilt his head back and slit his eyes against the invisible smoke that threatened to make them redden and water—chose this moment to present her with the last gift in his armoury: the photo romance he'd stolen from Mr. Papadopoulos's store so many years ago. It was still rolled up and thrust deep in his pocket.

"What's this?" asked Ruthie rudely.

"For you," said Sip. "I got it for you."

She took it gingerly, with the very tips of her fingers, as if doubting its provenance. But then she turned it over and examined it carefully: the glossy cover with the profile of the man and the woman leaning in for a slow kiss, and inside, more inky strips of photos telling of how those two had gotten to that kiss, but also, afterwards, of what had pulled them away from it again. Ruthie grasped the photo romance savagely and began to tear it apart. She wanted to tear that kiss right out of the world but failing that, any old chaos would do. The staples along the spine of the magazine caught at her fingers, but did she care? Soon wads of torn paper littered the surface of the water.

"Nothing, nothing!" shrieked Ruthie, as she snatched and tore. Something like that. And then over again and more of the same. The same words but fiercer; more paper in the air and on the water. Blood on her fingers where the staples went in.

And when the photo romance was gone entirely, divided equally into two phantom halves of a kiss, Ruthie looked down at her hands and was instantly calmed, as always, by the sight of her own blood.

From beneath his long childish lashes Sip watched her, fascinated. She sat on the cool concrete lip of the water reservoir tank rocking backwards and forwards and gnawing at her smeared fingertips. Should he offer her the box of chocolate cigarettes once again or would they suffer the same fate as the photo romance, pulled apart and pelted into the black waters? There was no telling with Ruthie; she was a world unto herself, and he the cold dark moon that circled but could never approach.

Nightwatching

"Well, Sip my little man," Ruthie began presently, "this has certainly been some strange summer." She hawked up a spitball and sent it into the reservoir. "Ayah, yes, *sir*, hottest summer in history, they say. And you know why, don't you? *Don't* you?"

Slowly Sip shook his head. He did not know why but then he did not suffer especially from the heat and certainly no more this summer than any other year. He was eight years old or perhaps nine, yet no year had been any hotter than the one before. Then he remembered Miriam, how she sat at the kitchen table tying and untying her doek so as to let her poor scalp breathe, or stood at the stove sighing and stirring and blowing down the front of her overalls.

"You don't know, do you, my little man," said Ruthie kindly. "You don't know why this summer is so hot that folks have been going around saying the end of the world is coming any minute—because the last days will be a relief, let me tell you, a bloody *relief*, compared to this everlasting heat."

It was true, Sip knew no such thing. He hadn't heard the talk, but then his father was a taciturn man except when drunk.

Ruthie searched the sky until she found a pale sliver of the unrisen moon rocking up and down on the horizon. "There," she cried. "Do you see that!"

Well, what of it, it was just the moon—surely she didn't care about the moon. His Ruthie, his sun.

"Now let me tell you about weather and the moon landing," Ruthie began gleefully, as if to say, *Do you mean to tell me, you ignorant boy, that you know nothing, know nothing, of the man in the moon and his wife made of green cheese and their children, also cheese?* But, after all, it was true: Sip knew nothing of such tales except that they required some mother to tell them.

Ruthie leaned forward, swinging her legs up and down as she spoke.

"There were these astronauts, see, from America. And they shot them up into outer space to see how far they could get to. Round about the moon, though, they ran out of, of food, so they had to come home. But the one, Mr. Neil Armstrong, he says to the others, 'Since we're here anyway, why don't we just get out for a while. Stretch our legs and look around.' Now the instructions were the opposite— President Kennedy, he's from America too, he saw them off and he said to them very clearly, 'You can go up and have a look around but don't touch anything.' But once you're in space it's like you're in another country so who cares what the president of the old one is saying. So these astronauts decide to land on the moon and a couple of them get out and jump up and down for a bit. Back on earth everyone is yelling, 'Get down, you fuckers!' And the president is pulling at his hair and shouting, 'What did I tell you about not touching anything, you bloody fools?'"

Ruthie took a breath, the first, it seemed, since she had begun. Sip was looking at her with flattering approbation. He didn't believe a word of her nonsense, but he was pleased as punch when she took the time to spin him a tale

"So, and so that's why the weather's changed. Because of the moon landing and all these damn astronauts jumping up and down as if it's a trampoline. You mark my words, young Sipho, it's only going to get hotter in summer and colder and colder in winter. I bet you anything you like we won't survive the decade. This planet will either freeze or burn to a bloody crisp. Any day now. Yessiree, any day now."

Ruthie was pleased with her rhetoric and hoped it had scared the pants off Sip. But when she slid her eyes sideways she saw that he was dreamily staring out at that pale rocking moon and every now and then nodding his head as if to say, *Uh-huh, funny old world* or—but this was much worse—*Funny old Ruthie, you daft girl, you crazy kid, you.*

Bloody! she thought. Anger suddenly had her in its jaws, shaking her from side to side. Her cheeks were hot and her chest burned and her armpits had begun to hum. It was red girl trying to get out again; it was that ugly red bitch bursting out of her skin. Well, let her, thought Ruthie and she grabbed Sip's arm. "Look!" But Sip was terrified of the water and reluctant to lean over the edge of the reservoir tank, though Ruthie craned and pointed and exclaimed and harried. So in the end she had to grab him and pull at him and then just plain drag him to the edge of the concrete lip and hold him with his head right out over the water until it was clear (it had always been clear) that there was nothing bobbing about in the tank but rage, her own murderous, buoyant rage.

What saved him was not crying. He never had, never would. If he'd sobbed or wailed she might have been overcome with disgust and dropped him like a stone into that tank. Or if he'd begged for mercy or yelled for help or struggled or whimpered or screamed. Might have. Who knows? She was just that mad and the sun was spasming closer with each pulse of her heart. Down below them in the grass the crickets were sliding the veld backwards and forwards between their dry insect thighs. Heat blasted up through the cracked earth and the sky was a tight blue noose falling over his head.

Sip looked into the water and saw his helplessness meet her hatred like two halves of a moon. Or his love, her rage. But he didn't cry although he wanted to and this wasn't because of his terror, which was considerable, but because Ruthie in his heart was dying—not dead yet, mark, not

Nightwatching

quite—and the pain of her demise was awful. He remained as still as he could, shutting just his eyes, until years had passed and he'd grown up and out of his small, pitiful self.

There was no way to survive the reservoir, Ruthie knew, even if you could swim, because the sides of the tank went straight up and they were slimy with years of greasy water and lichen growing halfway to the top. No stepladder either or any old thing to hold onto and the police had cut down the one hank of rope with its sun-bleached buoy when they'd taken up the last green kid. The way Ruthie figured it was you lasted as long as you kept swimming round and round like a rat in a bucket. And after that, treading water, and after that, drowned. She'd seen it before, or the results of it, at least, so in the end Ruthie pulled Sip back from the edge. Well, she'd been going to anyway, she was always going to. But then he just lay there in such a small boneless heap and with his face turned away from her.

"Hey," she yelled. "Hey, you!"

Sip didn't turn around. He was ashamed. Of himself, of her, of the day's bewildering sum of failures and how they all added up to this dizzying moment on the edge of the water tank with the concrete burning through the thin fabric of his shorts and the glare bouncing off the water in all directions. The air seemed to fizz like a carbonated drink. He turned aside and retched but nothing came up.

"Hey," yelled Ruthie again, and she jumped up and made her way to the stepladder, flinging first one leg and then the other over the railing. But she stopped abruptly before she disappeared and regarded him kindly.

"Come on, then," she coaxed, "we can go home together, if you like."

Sip shook his head; he would not turn around.

"You can ride on my handlebars," she clarified.

But he would not turn around. He pulled himself upright and sat with his legs clasped to his chest to give himself ballast. But he would not turn around and this was because of the unaccustomed water that had begun to bulge in his eyes. He was blinking rapidly, as fast as he could, and swallowing hard too, and he thought he'd soon see clearly again. But he would not turn around.

The bicycle was in its usual place under the privet hedge but pushed well back and out of the way of casual regard. The smart red sports car was still parked out front on the gravel sweep of drive with a couple of bags hoisted in the narrow back seat, which meant that the Guests must soon leave. Oh, why hadn't they yet? thought Ruthie from her sullen perch in the long grass of the back garden, where she was watching the wide lounge windows whose curtains

Nightwatching

had not yet been drawn against the dusk and the powdered moths and the hot, panting breath of evening.

Seeing the car parked in the driveway gave Ruthie an odd feeling, she could not say why. Yet it was his car, red and shiny, the gleaming outer form of his perfect emptiness. She wished she could tell someone about that car, Miriam perhaps, or Trudy Mason if they had still been friends. *No, Ruthie, man!* she could imagine Trudy Mason exclaiming, her hand over her mouth, and she didn't need Miriam to finish the rest of the sentence. *Ruthie, you silly girl, why are you climbing now into a car with a strange man?*

So that's where it had all begun, thought Ruthie. As if she hadn't known, for how many times had she not been warned? And done it still. The moon must have slipped behind a cloud, turning the outlines of things tremulous. It was just a car, wasn't it—it couldn't harm anyone.

From over the garden wall drifted the sound of piano music. First slow, then fast and loud and agitated. Oh Lord, she was at it again, thought Ruthie, rolling her eyes. Sometimes but not often, although always on a Sunday evening, the piano teacher would do her music. But hardly ever this loud and surely never this mean. The music was a live thing wriggling through the garden, a snake. Ruthie put her hands over her ears and leaned closer to the golden square of window imprinting itself on the moving shadows of the rhododendrons that clumped around the back porch. After a while her eyes adjusted and she could make out the three people inside the room—her dad and the two Guests, who were laughing and drinking from the good glasses again. Lena was in the middle, throwing back her head to show her slim, dark throat.

Her dad must have put on the gramophone then, because Lena began to dance around the room, holding her wineglass in the air and kicking off her high heels and grabbing first one man and then the other and spinning in a wild abandon of flaring skirt and flying hair. Was she wearing the charm bracelet? Ruthie couldn't see, although she thought she caught a glimpse of the gold necklace winking its strange message on and off like a street sign: *Live Love Laugh*. For a moment Lena tottered and appeared to fall but her dad caught her and pulled her into his lap. Suddenly the picture window seemed to detach itself from the darkness and fly off into the night, a golden cube of light, whirling.

Ruthie lay on her back and thought about where to go. Bleeker Street, maybe, or the park? But she was so tired, and hungry too. The light went on in the kitchen and Ruthie thought, Oh, Miriam! with a relief hardly to be borne. She wanted to lay her hot, tired head in Miriam's lap as she'd once done unthinkingly, before confusion and bewilderment entered her heart. But when she ran around to the side door and let herself into the kitchen she found Miriam sitting at the table with her head drooped upon her arms. She hardly even looked up when Ruthie came in except to say, "Where've you been all day, meisie?" Oh, what was wrong with everyone today?

There was a pot of water boiling on the stove, and beside Miriam a bowl of green peas waiting to be shelled, but supper was a mirage in the vanishing distance and Ruthie was setting no store at all by it. She cut herself a thick slice of bread and butter and then another. From the lounge came the sound of dance music and laughter, chairs sliding across parquet and a man's voice saying, "Well, sis, and when shall we announce the good news?" Ruthie was thirsty, too, and she didn't give a damn about the day of the week. She stood in the meagre yellow light from the fridge and tilted a bottle of Coca-Cola down her throat. Miriam looked up but she didn't admonish her and for some reason this evidence of neglect cut Ruthie to the quick. Well, okay then. So what? She leaned her head against the door and gulped at the sweet, harsh drink. But the taste of the Coca-Cola reminded her of the night before, and of the blue dust motes floating in the air and the stickiness of the brandy and Coke. She gagged and threw the bottle in the sink, where it broke against the edge, the liquid foaming up and frothing for a moment before swirling down the drain.

"Tcha, girl, what nonsense are you up to now?" But before Ruthie could answer, Miriam had already laid her weary head on her arms again.

The dance music coming from the other room was the kind Miriam hated and tried to jiggle out of the radio whenever it came on. Ruthie recognized Mr. Nat King Cole singing, ". . . fascination, I know . . . ," and wondered if it was this that was making Miriam so damn angry. Miriam hated Mr. Nat King Cole, *hated* him, and just plain refused to believe that a black man could make such a silly white noise. "No really," Ruthie had told her the first time they'd heard him on the radio, "I'll show you." And she'd found her dad's favourite record with Mr. Nat King Cole smiling away on the cover. But was Miriam grateful? No way, not a bit, not that one. "Shew weh!" she'd exclaimed, putting her hands up to her cheeks. Black face, white music! Miriam hardly ever fussed and she was never rude about things a person couldn't help like the colour of their skin, but that Nat King Cole really pulled her tail, so Ruthie made sure to grab the radio dial whenever he started in on his enchanted *blah blah blah* and his fascination *da da da* and his bewitched *dum de dum*.

But now, examining Miriam's slumped shoulders and bowed head, Ruthie wasn't even certain that she was hearing the dance music or the sounds of laughter and clinking glasses from the next room. The pot of water on the stove

Nightwatching

came to the boil but Miriam didn't stir so Ruthie began to shovel scoops of mielie meal into the rolling water. She had no very firm idea of how much meal to add to the pot so she counted out four heaped scoops then added another one for luck. Well, she was hungry and she didn't have a good feeling about supper.

"Come, Miri," she coaxed, "do you want me to help you with those peas?" When Miriam didn't move she grabbed the bowl and anxiously began squeezing the little green peas out of their pods. But she had no expertise in this new endeavour either and most of the shelled peas bounced this way and that across the oilcloth of the kitchen table or else remained stubbornly hooded in their pods. Bloody.

From the room next door Lena began tinkling her silver bells and saying, "Lionel, sweetie, you're dancing me off my feet again," and her dad laughed also and said something, but too softly to hear quite. Mr. Nat King Cole was singing, ". . . red sails in the sunset . . . ," and the brother was knocking with a fork on his wineglass and saying, "Ahem-hem, such good news, sis. Just wait." When he said this last thing, when he said "Just wait," he seemed to let all the air out of his lungs at once so that it sounded as if a wrong note had been struck in the melody of silver bells and red sails and ringing wineglasses that accompanied the couple dancing barefoot on the parquet floor.

"Hmm?" murmured Lena in a distracted sort of way. "Wat sê jy, nou, boet?" But it was plain that she'd heard it too, this missed beat.

"No, but luvvy, the aunties will want to throw a party for you, don't forget. A proper coolie send-off. Ag, and they'll want to meet young Blackburn over here. Show him some of that old Cape Coloured hospitality, hey."

Had there ever been a silence like it? The mielie pap on the stove bubbled over and a fly tumbled and drowned noisily in the dish of watermelon syrup on the windowsill. Slowly, Miriam raised her head from her arms and blew the air out of her cheeks. *Uh*-huh. As if to say, *Yup, yup, yebo.* As if to say, *Well, there was always something about that girl.* As if to say, *Ho, Coloured, you mean? Don't tell me.*

But she didn't say a thing, although she caught Ruthie's glance in the wide-eyed throwing. Caught and held and *hush-now*-ed. Then put her hand over her mouth to keep the laughter from spilling out. Motioned Ruthie to do the same.

But Ruthie wasn't laughing. Didn't feel remotely like it; no, there was no jauntiness in her at all. At first she didn't understand and then she thought she did and then once again understanding slid from her in all directions. She put her hand out to grasp the table's edge, not minding, for once, the stickiness of the oilcloth. The silence in the next room went on and on although it wasn't really silence because there was

Nightwatching

still dance music coming from the gramophone if one cared to listen. No one was, though. Listening. Of this Ruthie was certain. Miriam was still gasping, shaking like a great jelly on a plate. Then her father was saying something but she couldn't hear what because Lena was hollering blue murder and her brother was laughing like a drain. There was a slap and more dirty-water laughing and the brother's voice saying, "Ag, luvvy, you mean you haven't told him?" and another slap, but this one broken in half by a man's playful yelp and her father's voice saying, "Now then, you two, you must . . ."

The louder the noise around him—and this Ruthie knew from long experience—the louder the noise, the softer her dad spoke. And most times it worked, the room falling silent around him, because as he'd once told his daughter in a rare moment of telling her anything at all, the less one said, the more it counted. Well, okay. All right. But not today, obviously, because no one stopped yelling or even slowed down their yelling and now it sounded like the brother had begun on his everlasting tickling. Lena wasn't laughing, though, quite the opposite. Weeping, it sounded like, and struggling and shrieking.

"Oh, Lionel, tell him to stop it, man."

"Stop it!" yelled her dad. "Stop it, right now."

Oh, thought Ruthie, so she . . . no, but then he . . . But she couldn't finish her thought. She had hardly ever heard her dad yell, although she'd witnessed his anger. But his anger was a cold, just thing, as carefully weighed and judiciously measured as a spoonful of medicine poured out before bed to cure a child's fever. Miriam was looking at the open doorway with big eyes and straining forward to listen to the unaccustomed thunder of her father's righteousness. He had lifted the needle off the record but without his usual dexterity and a sharp breeze had clipped the sails of Mr. Nat King Cole's sunset.

"You two must behave yourselves. You're guests in this house," her dad was saying.

Something was different but she couldn't say what. Her dad wasn't yelling, he was speaking in his cold, medicinal voice. He was weighing his words and meting out justice. But Miriam heard it too. She put her chin in her hands and pursed her lips.

The music teacher left off playing her silly piano music that had been echoing through the dusk since the sudden quiet of the snatched-up record and the silence went bouncing about the kitchen like a rubber ball, hitting first one wall and then another. Ruthie put her hands over her ears.

"Come now, you two," her dad was saying when Ruthie eventually took her hands away from her ears.

Lena gave a shrill, cracked laugh and said, "Ag, Lionel, sweetie, don't listen to *him*, he's just . . . ," and then lots more about jealous this and crazy that, but Ruthie stopped listening because she was thinking about the something different that had entered the house on silent-pawed feet and when and why. But what it was she couldn't say quite. "You two," she repeated to herself, "you two, you two." And then, in a wondering sort of voice, as of someone who might wonder *picannin*? But it was not this word that she repeated but others that she had never heard before, although she only half understood them or the sense beneath them, at least: "A proper coolie send-off," she murmured, in something like admiration.

From the driveway came the sound of the sports car reversing furiously then shrieking hard and fast down the gravel road and into the red-eyed darkness. Her dad came to the door of the kitchen, shaking his head and saying, ". . . bloody driver. He'll be lucky if he makes it back to Bloem in one piece." He paused at the door but didn't come in, although he smiled vaguely at his daughter and offered her the coloured comic supplement from out of his Sunday newspaper before turning and walking away.

Miriam shrugged at his retreating back and went to the stove to peer into the pot of mielie pap. "Hai kona, girl." She whistled. "But why are you adding so much meal to the water? Tcha." Exasperated, she searched for a sheet of newspaper in which to empty the thick pot of hardened maize meal because surely no one would care to eat such dry and crusty pap. And how many times had that child watched her tilt a half cup of meal into the pot of boiling water? Where were her eyes? But Miriam couldn't be huffy for long because the to-do with that terrible Lena woman and her devil brother had cheered her up no end.

Half-breeds! she thought. And not an ounce of breeding between them, ha!

"Come here, girl," she called, beckoning to Ruthie, because it was about time someone showed that child how to make a decent pot of pap. About time and no better time to start than now. But when she turned around again the kitchen door was just swinging shut and the rustle of the privet hedge beneath the window was all there was to mark the fall of evening into night.

"Three days! Three? But why didn't you come sooner?" Miriam was beside herself.

Sip's father stood at the kitchen door with his cloth cap in his hands to say that Sip hadn't come home for three days. Also three nights, going on for four.

"Why did you not come sooner?" Miriam could only repeat herself. She stood with her hands on her hips and stamped her foot in frustration. But her anger at the boy's father was strained because, in truth, she hadn't noticed Sip's absence either. *Now, where . . . ?* she'd thought to herself once when dishing up meat stew for supper and, *Is that . . . ?* she'd wondered another time on hearing a small rattle of footsteps in the courtyard. But of Sip himself—Sip, the flesh-and-blood boy with his long child's lashes and his fastidious ways, Sip who cut out his patterns with his tongue poking to one side of his mouth and who sewed up his pieces of velvet and satin with tiny doll's stitches—of this Sip she had not given a thought.

Sip's father pulled his cloth cap inside out then back again. The cap in his big gardener's hands looked small and abused and Miriam wanted to snatch it from his grasp. "Come inside." She opened the door wider and beckoned him to sit at the kitchen table. But he wouldn't be drawn across the threshold. Never had, never would. He did not like to enter the houses of white folks, even by the back door, and this was more a matter of temperament than of the kind of work he did, which was gardens, mainly. So Miriam yanked off her apron and hurried outside to sit on the concrete steps of the courtyard so that he could tell her the rest of the story.

But it turned out there was nothing else to say. Sip's father cleared his throat once. Twice. Looked up, looked down. There was nothing else to say.

"So you say you saw him when?" asked Miriam. At ten

in the morning there was no shade to speak of in the concrete courtyard. The light hurtled down and spun off the walls. The light sought her out like a bad conscience or the Lord's voice in her ear saying, *When, Miriam? When?* She put her hand to her eyes to cut the glare and tried to think. Three days ago? Four? There'd been no Sip during the weekend when the guests had come to stay. But before?

Sip's father thought Saturday night. Couldn't be sure but thought so. He pulled and pulled at his cap.

Drunkard, thought Miriam. She could smell it on him even now, the beer that had sweated through his skin for all these years, though he swore he hadn't had a mouthful of anything stronger than tea since Sunday morning. His nails were thick and ridged with the dirt of garden soil and the whites of his eyes were an oily yellow colour. Some days Sip winced when he sat down and when Miriam asked him what was wrong he pretended not to hear her. Or said nothing, and stared at her from beneath his lashes and smiled a little kind smile as if to say, *Not to worry, my Miriam, not to worry your head about me.* But mostly he pretended not to hear in the way of small, contrary boys, and Miriam, who'd had two small boys of her own and didn't like to trespass upon the solemn privacies of childhood, had stared down upon the child's nape between his sticking-out ears and pulled back the hand she had half reached out to touch him.

"But Sunday he was gone?" asked Miriam. "*All day Sunday?*"

Sip's father nodded. To the best of his recollection it was so, although his recollection was not at its best on Sunday, which was a befuddled torment of a day, usually, that left him high and dry, washed up on the shores of inebriation and remorse. Friday was payday and between Friday night's thirst and Saturday night's revelry Sip's father was hard pressed to account for his son's wavering presence. Shadows played against the whitewashed walls of the concrete room until it was difficult to tell if the child was real or ghost.

"We must go to the police," said Miriam. Then, when his vehement head-shaking had slowed down: "Well, what can we do?" In fact, she too shrank from such a course of action. The police whom she always thought of as a collective group, as a formation of khaki-uniformed men with bristle-cut hair marching in lockstep down the main road of the town with mirrored sunglasses shading their blank eyes. Guns, truncheons. *And what about tear gas?* her son would have said. *And what about dogs?*

Jericho, Jericho. Her heart yearned after him. He was the source of her distraction and her sorrow. She hadn't heard from him in days.

"Well, or what about Mr. Blackburn? We must tell him about Sip and ask him what to do. His advice." Miriam was so relieved at this solution that she could have cried. Almost did, and then—thinking of the poor lost child, God alone knew where he was—did, a little. Caught herself up, tried to wipe her eyes on the corner of her apron but found herself snatching uselessly at her overall and remembered the apron still swinging on the peg behind the kitchen door. She took a deep breath and smoothed the cheap fabric of her overall across her knees.

"Tonight when he comes home I will ask for his advice," she promised. "He will tell us what to do next and if—*if* we must go to the police perhaps he can speak for us."

Yes, it was by far the best solution, thought Miriam. And Mr. Blackburn, though often hungry when he came home and anxious to hear the evening's news on the radio, was relaxed by the end of supper, his good humour restored. *Thank you, Miriam,* he might say, *those cutlets were done to a tee.* Or he would ask Ruthie to play him her piano exercises, lying back in his armchair in the lounge with a bemused expression on his face while the girl banged out her terrible wrong notes as if she were typing up an angry letter.

"I'll ask him tonight, after supper," resolved Miriam. "But maybe the boy will be back by then. He may be back anytime now, you know. We mustn't lose hope."

She shielded her eyes so that she could look up into the light that seemed to strike off the concrete walls of the courtyard like sparks from a story. Even just one of those sparks could kill you.

Ruthie was sitting as still as she could in the shade of the eucalyptus tree beside the reservoir. She was sitting still and thinking about herself sitting as still as she could in the shade of the eucalyptus tree. More and more that summer Ruthie would ambush herself with these thoughts, thoughts that put into unnecessary words the girl who was sitting or watching or cycling or whistling, just passing time, and suddenly words would pop out of her head like a thought bubble in the Sunday comic supplement and there she'd be: Ruthie sitting. It was like living her life twice; it was like glimpsing herself in the room of a house she'd watched many times before.

In the shade of the eucalyptus tree beside the water reservoir, she began again. When she was anxious or frightened, as she was now, it soothed her to imagine a correspondence between her self and her thoughts, her waywardness and the stern, unwavering girl she yearned to be. Some days "Ozymandias" helped but mostly not, and anything was better than the ragged itch of *I wish . . . I want . . . I will . . .* It was only self-consciousness but it felt like a homecoming at those times when she briefly coincided with herself—when she idly watched herself sit, half dreaming, or saw herself gazing out into the middle distance. But more often the summer cracked open and each day a little more.

Sip was gone, they said, had been for three days. Since the weekend, that was. Had she been the last to see him? His head turned away from her as she climbed over the railing of the reservoir? The fact was, Ruthie knew that Sip was gone because she'd been looking for him. Just here and there, just now and then. At first her conscience smote her—"Smote, smote, smote," she whispered in the odd corners of her day where she kept expecting to come upon him. And later, after the Guests roared off, she'd wanted to tell him about the secret things she'd learned. *A proper coolie send-off*—it was a small gift to lay at his feet, for no one thought to give Sip anything, though he was generous to a fault. Ruthie shook her head resolutely. She didn't like to think of the photo romance or the chocolate cigarettes he'd brought her. She didn't like to think of his thin wrists twisted in her hands. But mostly she didn't like to think of the hunger that lived inside her and the hunger that lived in the water and how, for a moment, Sip had gotten between them.

Ruthie sniffed the air cautiously. There was a smell like coughing that was eucalyptus leaves and then the thick oily smell of the eucalyptus bark that, at the end of a hot summer like this one, would often burst into sudden loud fire. *Bang,*

bang, bang, three black trees burning up, just like that. And there was a deeper staleness in the air that Ruthie recognized as summer running out. The grass was turning brown in patches and the leaves on the trees had a moth-eaten, threadbare look. It wasn't autumn yet, that was for damn sure, but summer's green fuse had burned clear through and now the faint smell of electricity was on the wind.

But she couldn't smell the rotten kid stink yet so she stood up quickly. The stepladder was still down because it had only been three days. No one ever checked the abandoned reservoir or hardly ever, and even then. Ruthie grabbed the bottom rung and hoisted herself up. For a moment when her feet left the ground she had the strangest feeling that she'd been here before, in this very moment, but the picture that came to mind wasn't the water tank up whose steep sides she and Sip had pulled each other but the veld outside the house on Bleeker Street where she'd crouched, with the grass itching the back of her knees, while the terrible woman yanked and yanked at poor old Sip.

What a kid he was for trouble, she thought. What a bloody nuisance he was. But she couldn't help smiling, and it was often the case that when not actually in the presence of his puppy-ish regard and shyly raised hello-fingers, the mere remembrance of his devotion would warm her lonely heart.

All the same she could barely breathe. The sky was

white like the last frame in a movie and the wind was making a snapping sound as if a piece of film had gotten caught in the projector. When she looked up she could hardly see the top of the reservoir. There was nothing for it, though, so Ruthie gave herself a hard shake, a shake as if to say, *Looks like this is it, girl, looks like this is the end of the damn movie.* The words meant nothing; they were just words and the wind dispersed them and pretty soon she began the long scramble upwards.

She hardly knew how long it took to climb to the top of the water tank: hand over hand, one foot after the other, her thoughts suspended in vertical time. But when she found the railing and flung herself over the top to reach the concrete lip beyond, all the worries she'd left behind in the shade of the eucalyptus were waiting to meet her. *Bang! Bang! Bang!* Oily flames roared skywards.

Sip was not in the water tank, no siree. But where then? Where was that boy? He was a creature who frustrated expectation at every turn, and the relief that Ruthie momentarily felt at not finding his small self slopping about down in the water—as he had, for three days, slopped about in the bilious waters of her imagination—ceased abruptly.

Where was he then? Oh, where was that boy?

Ruthie sat down slowly with her knees drawn up to her chest and began to bite at her wrist. And it was not the

Nightwatching

end of the movie, turned out, but only somewhere in the middle, the terrible white sky playing on a continuous loop around her. Over and over again.

There was a story about pigs that Jericho liked to tell her but Miriam was in such a state she could not now remember what these pigs did or thought or accomplished. They had begun as farm animals and then they'd decided to walk upright and that was when the trouble began. "All animals are equal," Jericho was fond of saying to illustrate this injustice or that outrage; "all animals are equal but some animals are more equal than others!" "Ho, why don't you speak plainly," his brother would mock, "are we all animals, then, in this country?" "This is what I'm trying to tell you," Jericho would say, "to explain once again why some animals, some animals . . ." Recalling how the rickety kitchen table in Thabong Township would rock backwards and forwards across the stiff and resolute legs of her quarrelling sons, Miriam put her hands to her head. Only this morning, Jonas had come to tell her that Jericho had received orders to leave—he was already across the border. But he sent his mother all his love, his warmest love.

"Oh, where . . . ?" she cried, her knuckles pressed against her teeth.

"Probably Angola," Jonas whispered. "Hush now."

Miriam put her head in her hands to try to cup the unfamiliar despair.

As for Temperance Thandile, she too had gone to ground. It was the opposite of Jericho because her mother knew very well where her daughter had disappeared to, although she received neither phone call nor letter to confirm her suspicions and neither did she expect to. The child had gone off to live with Harry Ditsebe in a rented room on the Location. That was all there was to it. And "perhaps one day" was all her mother had to hope for in the way of Milo-eyed babies or a daughter returned to her.

"Hush now, Mama," Jonas whispered again, "you know you mustn't . . ."

Of course she knew. Now that she was the mother of a freedom fighter there was nothing she did not know of secrecy and subterfuge. But about those pigs, the four-legged and the two, Miriam found herself strangely confused, not to say preoccupied. It was as if they had found a border in her mind to lumber around, grunting and truffling their snouts in the dirt.

"Three days, now. *Three!* Why didn't you come sooner?" Mr. Blackburn had asked, pushing away his newspaper and going straight away to phone the police. And afterwards he'd stood at the little phone table out in the hall, tapping

Nightwatching

a pencil against his teeth and thinking hard. But when he turned around again, she would not catch his eye, she would not look up, no, not even when he cleared his throat to say, "And the mother is, she is . . . ?" How should I know where the mother is, thought Miriam, am I the world's mother that I must always be keeping track of this lost boy, that contrary girl? This freedom-fighter son, that pregnant-too-soon daughter? But she said nothing, there was nothing to say.

Miriam sat at the kitchen table and turned over a loose scrap of velvet in her fingers. Sip was careful with his material, gathering up his satins and wisps of lace, his rayons and his fragments of bright silk. But somehow this scrap of fraying blue velvet had escaped his thrifty gaze and fallen between the legs of a kitchen chair. She'd saved it up; she was saving it still. If she kept it safe to return to him, he would be kept safe to be returned to them, she told herself. She wasn't usually sympathetic to this sort of magic but she was anxious and tired and her mind had hitched itself to a mulish circle of guilt and *why not* and *what if* and *when, when, when*, so that it was all she could do to keep still.

Once more she agitated the velvet in her hands, turning it over and over, and hardly glanced up when she heard the front door open then slam shut again with barely a pause for breath. Ruthie. The girl went directly to the music room and knocked back the lid of the piano then clattered her stool across the parquet floor and straight away began to break her "Chopsticks" across the keys.

The terrible sound of Ruthie's piano playing didn't usually rile Miriam. Quite the contrary. Most days *when* she could coax the child to sit at her practice she would smile to think of the music teacher's dismay, for she was no admirer of Bettina Foley and could recognize malevolence from farther away than the music teacher's neatly curtained, prettily fenced bungalow. But today the noise was unbearable, though there was no question but that she must bear it. She closed her eyes and held on tightly to the square of velvet. It was a flimsy thing and threadbare in her hands. Miriam imagined the piano keys stretched out like a row of teeth bared in an endless rictus grin and with each *da da da dada* Ruthie knocked and punched at them. And then as suddenly as it began, it ended. All at once Ruthie slammed down the lid, dislodging a silver-framed photograph of her mama that had stood for so long on top of the piano that Ruthie had all but forgotten its existence. Running in to forestall disaster, Miriam saw that the photograph of the faintly smiling woman had fallen onto the parquet floor, although its glass had not shattered. Miriam stood for a moment, tapping her foot and tutting as Ruthie, chagrined, restored the photograph to its place.

"Humba, child," Miriam murmured, turning her back

Nightwatching

and making for her chair at the kitchen table. But the girl followed close upon her heels.

"Miri," Ruthie coaxed, standing first on one leg and then on the other. She hadn't stood so since she was a child—what was the girl up to?

Miriam leaned her cheek on her hand and looked at her. Ruthie was flushed as if she'd been riding her bike hard and for some time. Or was it the piano? No, surely not. Her denim shorts seemed to have shrunk in the wash again because they rode up high on her hips and her legs protruded from them, long and thin and dirty. What a girl she was for growing out of things, Miriam thought, her canvas tennis shoes broken down at the heel and her blouse gaping tight across the chest. She'd been a sturdy, compact child with a child's unsinkable resolve, but now she teetered and overbalanced with every gust of wind that blew her way.

". . . not chicken again, *please*, Miri." Ruthie was chattering on about supper. "And not meat loaf or cutlet or . . . and absolutely no chicken again, okay? But why not eggs?" she sang out. "Eggs would be delicious tonight. Simply grand."

Ruthie was always trying to persuade Miriam to scramble eggs for supper. It was her dearest wish and one that had gone sadly unfulfilled until now. Suddenly Miriam lost patience with her. She leaned forward and thumped the table hard. "*Why* are you thinking about your stomach, girl?

Are you so worried about what to eat and what not to eat that you have forgotten about your friend?"

"Don't say that, Miri, Sip was never my friend," said Ruthie, teasing. She laughed when she saw Miriam's outraged face and the more she laughed the harder the new laughter came to chase down the old. Oh, she didn't think she could stop!

Miriam was no longer angry. She'd seen this sort of thing before and how many times, for didn't she have a daughter of her own, a girl who, in her time, had cried and laughed and wailed and danced, one emotion following the next with the rapidity of water flowing into water. Ai kona, but she was tired. And she purely did not feel like Ruthie's nonsense tonight. The pigs that had been trundling all day around the rim of her mind in a ragged, weary circle snorted and rolled over in the mud.

"Oh, Miriam," said Ruthie, suddenly contrite, "don't be like that. Don't be sad about, about him. He's . . . that Sip, he's, he's just . . ."

Ruthie thought for a moment but nothing came to her except a conviction, sudden and unshakeable, that Sip was safe somewhere. Out of sight, inexplicably detained, hopelessly unpunctual, he'd appear again, as innocent of explanation as the wind. Ruthie had gone to the reservoir. She had been a child, a mere *kid* when she'd set out but she'd returned, triumphantly, a woman. And with a woman's conviction of the world's discordant fidelities. To her everlasting relief there had been no green stink-kid in the water reservoir, no body buoyant on its own rottenness half rising to meet her despair. The discovery had filled her with joy.

On the way home she'd cycled as hard as she could along the shoulder of the highway, hunching her back into the wind and enjoying the indignation of passing motorists who flicked their lights at her and hooted or threw empty beer bottles and yelled blurred obscenities from hastily cranked windows. "Yah, yah! Fuck off, kid!" someone cat-called. Someone else wolf-whistled. Suddenly she felt strong and as powerful as a machine, as if the bicycle she rode were an extension of her legs, her muscles, her will. The stale beery breath of summer fluttered up into her face in a fug of exhaust fumes and dust and hot tar but she just pedalled until the wind that came up off the highway blew too fast to smell of anything but the end of times, the ashes of the dying season and this poor crazy summer that had finally cracked clean in half.

"Come on, Miri." She spoke soothingly now for something in her, too, had given way, an old achy hurt, and she felt full of the milk of human kindness. "Come on, Miri, old thing, I'm sorry I've gone and upset you, but look here, why don't I fix us up a bite to eat. Hmm? You just sit there, Miri, you sit there and watch and say if I'm doing anything wrong."

She had already snatched up eight eggs and was cracking them, willy-nilly, into a bowl, splashing in milk by the pint and beating up the whole gluey mess with clumsy enthusiasm. Miriam didn't like to see her so near the stove but neither had she the heart to spoil the girl's fun, so she only murmured "No, no, too hot" when Ruthie turned the plate to its highest mark, and yanked her back from the splatter of butter.

And, yes, the eggs were burnt, somewhat, brown at the edges and curdled, a little, at the centre. But Miriam ate her share with a smile and Ruthie with a bigger one. And they were not contrived smiles, neither one. For when had anyone last made Miriam a meal and when had Ruthie ever eaten scrambled eggs for supper?

Annemarie Willems had enjoyed the Saturday afternoon matinee, but her good friend, Bettina Foley, most assuredly had not. A poor man's Paul Newman, she complained of its leading man, Mr. Steve McQueen, and nothing could move her from this original pronouncement, not that Annemarie even attempted to do so, for her friend was not one to twitch like a newly caught fish at the end of her opinions. Oh no, not Bettina, who had welcomed the earliest cast of autumn

Nightwatching

in the air with a new twin-set from Kurtz Fashions in town. Now, settling her cardigan more firmly about her shoulders, she offered to treat her friend to a cup of tea and a slice of melktert at Ouma's Tearoom. There was lots of time, wasn't there, and she had so much news to tell.

Annemarie was all ears. Was it about that handsome Mr. Blackburn? she wondered. Already certain rumours had begun to circulate through the town, but natuurlik she would rather hear about matters from the horse's mouth. Harrumphing slightly at the indignity of the comparison, Bettina was nevertheless gratified. For who knew more about the scandal next door than the next-door neighbour? And, truly, this wasn't through any untoward eavesdropping on her part, Annemarie knew—who better?—that she desired nothing more passionately than peace and quiet and to keep herself to herself unless otherwise invited. But the uproar, hemel!—never had she heard such language and such screeching of tires, well!

"Wragtig?" Annemarie leaned forward again. "Ag, tell me everything, Tina."

But Bettina made her wait until they had been served the little aluminum pots of tea with their badly fitting lids through which the heat always escaped. And the two generous triangles of melktert, the best in town, wobbling slightly because they were still warm from the oven. "And now?" she asked the waitress rudely, "aren't you forgetting something?" The ousie wandered off in search of cake forks, jugs of milk, serviettes. Who knew what else she'd forgotten. As she walked away her hips knocked casually against jutting tables and chairs, the odd patron with a cup of tea half raised to her mouth. Tcha, thought Bettina, and these are the people who . . . who . . . Words deserted her.

Annemarie settled back in her chair. When Bettina got into one of her moods there was no talking to her. It was Annemarie Willems's privately held belief that her friend was a little too conscientious when it came to pulling in the grommets of her Warner's deluxe two-way and that this, this un*nat*ural constraint, while keeping her attendant to the music she played and the lessons she taught, was the cause of much of her tart huffiness. But the strong, sweet tea rallied Bettina and she set her cup with a precise clack upon its saucer, as of one moving a chess piece.

"But they were already engaged by then. Don't tell me you didn't know. He took her out dancing on Saturday night and Lord knows where the brother went. But one thing I *will* say, one thing: she's quite a pretty little thing. They often are, you know. Who? Man, *those* people, the Coloureds. Yes—*yes*, that's what I'm trying to tell you. That's what the fight was about on Sunday night. Yelling and screaming and glasses breaking then the two of them roaring off into the sunset. Ag no, man, not *him*, not Mr. B, natuurlik. Have you ever heard a cross word come out of his mouth? No, but the other two, that tramp and her brother—if he *is* her brother," concluded Bettina somewhat breathlessly.

"Hemel!" Annemarie threw up her hands in gratifying pantomime of her friend's dismay. Some of this she'd known but most not, and all of it was agreeably scandalous. It would be something to share with her lover, because Dot Priestly had been ill and housebound for so long that she had begun to take an uncharacteristic interest in the doings of her neighbours and the gossip of the small town.

"And what about—?" Annemarie paused delicately because Ruthie Blackburn with her wooden fingers and her tin ear was no favourite of her music teacher.

She need not have worried.

"Tcha, poor thing," murmured Bettina. "Poor motherless child—no one to look after her except that fat ousie in the kitchen. Why, do you know what I heard from my friend, Mrs. Kurtz?" She leaned across the table towards Annemarie until their heads were almost touching and whispered rapidly in her ear. Every now and then one or other of the women would let a sly giggle escape from between the fingers of a hand brought up to staunch a less-ladylike guffaw.

But it was getting on. Tea time was nearly over and

from the kitchen came the clatter of dishes in the sink and the strangely melancholic jazz on the African radio station. *Well*, Bettina raised her eyebrows delicately as if to say, *don't worry, we know when we're not wanted.*

"Ag, don't worry, juffie, we still have plenty of time to get back home," Bettina reassured her friend, who had recently purchased a television set and didn't like to be so much as five minutes late for the start of programming.

As it happened she was mistaken, for there was a roadblock out on the highway with a couple of police cars drawn up sideways on the shoulder. Two whole lanes were closed and cars crawled past in single file, flashing their lights and hooting while their occupants craned and gawped. But there was nothing to see so Bettina rolled down her window and inquired of the sergeant who was directing traffic through the melee what the trouble seemed to be. Annemarie had to admire her cheek.

The sergeant blinked but he was used to obeying his superiors.

"It's nothing to be concerned about, ma'am," he said. "Looks like some picannin got himself run over last week. Bloody Afs. Little fellow, too," the sergeant continued, because he had been moved, despite himself, by the small body flung sideways into the drainage ditch at the side of the road. It had been difficult, at first, to see what the

Nightwatching

trouble was but when the flies rose in a bright shimmering hum they'd found the child with the terrible gash through his breast. One arm almost severed, small hands clasped tight. Bending closer—despite the stink—his father's heart knocking against apprehension, the sergeant imagined that the boy had once been an appealing little chap. At least he thought he'd been. It was difficult to tell; death had swooped down and tossed him like a piece of rubbish by the side of the highway.

For a moment the sergeant had gazed down at the child's body and imagined those wide-open eyes staring into the blaze of his oncoming death. What a strange thing to do—he wasn't an imaginative man. It was just the effect of the small body under the high, whirling sky, the cars streaming past, the small hands that had been clasped as if in supplication.

Ag, but what could you do? What was the mother thinking, letting such a little chap play in the traffic? The sergeant shrugged in an effort to distance himself from the whole bloody mess and Bettina shook her head as if to marvel at such carelessness. But Annemarie was moved to ask when the accident had taken place.

"Five, maybe six days ago. Sunday evening, must have been. Fast car coming down the highway. Didn't see him, didn't stop." The sergeant shrugged. Life.

The line of cars behind them began to hoot again so

Bettina rolled up her window and moved on. For a while there was silence in the car as each woman considered the death of the picannin. Annemarie felt a sore place in her heart, ag, such a waste. They were passing the Greek Caffy and she glimpsed, for a moment, the Greek in his window. He was bent over his cash register as she had so often seen him before, late in the evening when all the other shops had closed for the night. She did not care for the old Greek. But at this moment, with his stoop and his frown and his soulful Hellenic eyes, he was the essence of all that was melancholy in the world. Annemarie had a sudden fancy that the Greek, of all the people in the small prairie town, was the picannin's true mourner.

Bettina drove slowly, making much of each turn and twist in the road as if trying to work out a puzzle in her mind. She was not fond of children, of black children in particular, and yet this ragged edge of highway, the darkness falling as it did, in this part of the world, with such needless emphasis, affected her strangely. A lonely sort of death, she couldn't help thinking, the picannin five days cold on the edge of the highway. Ah, but we are all alone when we die, she thought, then sagely batted the thought away.

She wondered if Annemarie would invite her in to an early supper and a couple of hours of television-watching, but knew she wouldn't. It was because of Annemarie's friend,

Nightwatching

that terrible librarian. There was no love lost between the two women, but what of it? She, Bettina Foley, was content to live alone with her music and her pupils, the cold clean harmony of her days, and, in time, for she was a realist, she would face the blessed counter-harmony of her death. But on the drive home from Bleeker Street, down Tesla and up Delmont and all along Unicor Road she noticed, in windows and through curtains, that flickering blue light of transmission around which others warmed their collective lives as at an ancient, prehistoric flame.